He put his shoulder to the door's edge and jerked. It flew open suddenly, revealing the bare-walled bedroom beyond.

'There you go, squire.' He grinned and tossed back a lank strand of fair hair. 'What do you think?'

Andy had been warned that it was unwise to take any accommodation in Walford without seeing it first, but it looked like he'd been lucky here. He walked into the room and put down his bags by the single bed.

'Not bad,' he murmured . . .

By the same author

The Outsider
The Dark Side of the Sun

EastEnders Novels

Home Fires Burning
Swings and Roundabouts
Flower of Albert Square

HUGH MILLER

Good Intentions

EastEnders – Book 3

By arrangement with the
British Broadcasting Corporation

GRAFTON BOOKS

A Division of the Collins Publishing Group

LONDON GLASGOW
TORONTO SYDNEY AUCKLAND

Grafton Books
A Division of the Collins Publishing Group
8 Grafton Street, London W1X 3LA

A Grafton Paperback Original 1986

ISBN 0-586-06811-2

Printed and bound in Great Britain by
Collins, Glasgow

Set in Times

Life has taught us that love
does not consist in gazing
at each other but in looking
outward together in the
same direction.

Saint-Exupéry

1

When the train had curved away from the platform and they could no longer see the arm waving from the carriage window, the couple turned and looked at each other.

'Well then. That's him away.' Jenny's eyes were filmed with tears but she was hanging on to her smile.

Her husband looked openly sad. 'Did he pick up the sandwiches off the kitchen table?'

'Aye. And the flask.'

They turned and faced the broad concourse of Glasgow Central Station. 'It's going to be odd, not having him about the place,' Jenny said.

'We'll just have to get used to that.' Tom peered through the criss-crossing throng of people. 'There's a buffet over there. Come on, we'll have a cup of tea.'

After queueing for nearly five minutes and deciding, in the meantime, to have a cream doughnut too, they found a table near the window. Tom set the tray down carefully while Jenny fitted herself into the unyielding plastic of the anchored seat.

'He said he'd write as soon as he got fixed up with proper digs.' Jenny reached in her coat pocket and took out the slip of paper with the address where he could be reached meanwhile:

NURSING STAFF RESIDENCY
KING GEORGE VI GENERAL HOSPITAL
ARMITAGE ROAD
WALFORD
LONDON E20

'I hope he likes it there.' She put the paper back in her pocket with such care that it might have been a precious talisman.

'I'm sure he will,' Tom said gruffly. 'Drink your tea while it's hot.'

In a city where it was practically taboo to express affection or sadness openly, the farewell to Andy had put a severe strain on Tom. He had wanted to put his arms around the boy, to kiss him in fact, but he had left that extravagance to Jenny and restricted himself to a tight, prolonged handshake.

Now, watching Jenny toying with her teacup, he wished he *had* kissed his foster-son and put a bear-hug on him into the bargain. Tom would never tell Jenny, but he was going to miss that young man more than the three who had already left home. And they were his own natural children.

'Twelve years went awful fast,' Jenny sighed.

'Aye, right enough.'

Andy O'Brien had come to them when he was thirteen. They were his fourth set of foster-parents and he stayed with them long past the time they had secretly feared he would leave.

'Just think, Tom. If it hadn't been for the shortage of nursing jobs in Scotland . . .'

'I know,' Tom murmured patiently. 'He might have stayed on with us another year or two. You've said that a few times this past fortnight.' He pointed to the doughnut in front of Jenny, its blob of cream waxy and deathlike in the fluorescent light. 'Eat that up, eh? It'll make you feel better.'

Jenny took a tiny bite and chewed on it as if it were bone-dry. She swallowed some tea and showed Tom her tenacious smile again. 'I was just thinking about the time he qualified. That was some party, eh?'

'Best we've ever had in our house.' Music and laughter, Tom remembered, carefree talk and the enveloping warmth of young people and their happiness. 'The colour of Andy's face when that wee student nurse kissed him.' Tom shook his head, smiling. 'He was always shy with the lassies.'

'And good-mannered with them, Tom. He was never less than a gentleman to the girls.'

Tom stared at his wife for a moment.

'What is it?'

'We've started talking about him as if he'd been away for ages.'

Jenny pushed the doughnut to the centre of the table. 'It feels like that already,' she said. Her smile had gone.

Ten minutes later they emerged into the brooding purple-grey light of Union Street. Rain clouds were banking down beyond the river, getting ready to move across the city and drench it. Jenny and Tom stood on the pavement sniffing the air, wondering what they should do now. They looked like any other middle-aged, comfortably-off, near-enough middle-class Glasgow couple. But standing on that cold street they felt different; it was as if they had been isolated from the rhythm of the life around them. They felt abandoned.

'Would ye like a walk round the shops?' Tom said.

Jenny thought about it, then nodded. 'We can go to Boots and Lewis's. There's one or two things I'm needing.'

'And Burton's. I fancy trying on some sports jackets.'

The decision taken, they moved off along the street. Tom whistled softly, no tune at all, just a tinselly cover for his gloom. Jenny walked with her eyes down, her face

9

expressionless. She was glad it would be an hour or more before they went home. It might be long enough for her to gain the strength to hold back her tears when she saw Andy's empty room.

2

Sister Meldrum's desk, like the rest of the office, was unnaturally tidy. There was the day book, some meticulously stacked folders, a tub with two pens and a pencil, a squat green telephone and nothing else but the unspotted expanse of polished wood.

'Sit down, Nurse O'Brien,' Sister said. Her Highland accent was dilute but unmistakable. She watched gravely as the tall, athletic-looking young man took the chair opposite her. 'I've been going over your papers.'

Andy nodded, trying to display the professional aplomb that would match his record. Sister's eyes hardened a shade, driving his gaze on to the desk. Tidy desks made him nervous. So did little women like Sister Meldrum.

'As nursing credentials go, I'd say yours are fine. Excellent, in fact.'

'Thank you,' Andy murmured. He tried to smile again, but she obviously didn't like · that. Maybe she found smiling untidy.

'But the record tells me nothing about yourself.' She made a testy mouth. 'About the kind of nurse you are in practice – about the qualities you bring to your work.'

'I don't suppose it does, no . . .' Andy cleared his throat.

'So I'll be keeping a close eye on you for a few days.'

'Of course.'

Sister shifted in her chair. Her expression shifted too, from dourly mistrustful to merely disapproving. It was as if his existence broke some rule or other. 'I have a reputation for being strict,' she said. 'It's a reputation I work hard to keep. Like yourself, I was trained in Glasgow and I was taught the value of standards – and the absolute necessity to maintain them.'

Andy had been told they were always worse when they left Scotland. Sisters, tutors, the old-time matrons, all dead keen to put muscles on their despotism the minute they crossed the border.

'I daresay you've worked under a strict Sister or two in your time, O'Brien.'

'One or two, Sister.'

'They should all be that way,' she snapped. 'Half the trouble in the hospital service these days is brought about by lax administration. *Enlightened* administration, they call it.' She sniffed. 'You'll find none of that nonsense on this ward.'

One of the little tyrants Andy had suffered under had been very much like Sister Meldrum, if his gauge of this woman was accurate. There were certainly physical similarities. Both had pillow-shaped little bodies and each, in the words of a nursing friend of Andy's, had a face like a hen looking through a bottle.

Sister peered at her watch. 'Staff Nurse Reilly will be along in a minute to take you round and explain your duties. Now listen.' She leaned forward, her face telling him she had a vital point to make. 'You'll both have identical rank on the record and on the ward, but for the time being I will regard Reilly as being senior.'

He hadn't expected anything else. In this profession, dominated as it was by women, a man had to prove himself every inch of the way.

'Before Staff gets here I want to make a couple of things clear.'

Andy tried to look receptive without seeming too submissive.

'Punctuality. I insist on it and I don't accept any excuses for bad time-keeping.' She waggled her head briefly, as if to underline what she had said. 'Ward discipline is something else I must have. None of this singing-while-you-work business, no slouching, no re-arranging of procedures to suit yourself. And record-keeping – it must be neat and thorough. Have you got all that?'

'Yes Sister.' It was a long time since he had been talked to like a green kid. She had mentioned nothing, so far, that hadn't been second-nature with him for years.

'Now.' The small face became grave again. 'There is one particular point of discipline I enforce harder than any other. No male nurse will fraternize with the female staff while they are on duty and under my supervision. I'm sure you know what I mean.' After a stern pause she added, 'I come down hard on any violation of that rule.'

At least she hadn't automatically assumed he was a poof. That was something. Andy was about to issue his assurances about leaving the girls alone when the door was tapped and opened.

'Ah.' Sister stood up and flicked a finger at Andy, indicating he should do the same. 'Staff Nurse Reilly, this is Staff Nurse O'Brien.'

As Andy rose he found himself confronting a short, dark-haired young woman with vivid blue eyes and a tight, professional smile. He was about to extend his hand then checked himself. In Sister's book that might be fraternisation. Instead he nodded and mumbled a hello.

'How do you do,' Staff Nurse Reilly said. Her voice was as crisply competent as her smile. She switched her eyes to Sister. 'Shall I take him round the ward now and show him the ropes?'

'Please.' Sister came to the door behind Andy. He could feel her presence, a dumpy threat. 'You won't forget what I've said, now?'

'No, Sister.'

'And one other thing . . .' The phrase had the effect of making Staff Nurse Reilly step outside and walk away a few paces, giving renewed privacy to Andy and the Sister. 'I hope you won't assume,' the little woman murmured, 'just because we have our nationality and training background in common, that you'll enjoy any special consideration or privileges while you're on my ward.'

'Of course not, Sister.'

As the door closed behind Andy he stared at Staff Nurse Reilly. She stared back, then moved off in the direction of the ward. Andy followed her, determined to find out, and fast, if she was anything like the Sister. If she was, he would seriously consider asking for a transfer.

At eleven o'clock a junior nurse came into the ward and told Andy he was wanted in the sluice room. He finished putting a dressing on a little girl's arm and went out into the passage, trying to remember which door led to the sluice.

When he located it he found Staff Nurse Reilly sitting on the work top swinging her legs. She was puffing on a cigarette with the kind of relish most people reserve for food. As Andy closed the door she pointed to an electric coffee pot beside her.

'Help yourself. There's milk in the jug and sugar in that jar.' She held out her packet. 'Fag?'

'No thanks.' Andy poured himself some coffee and wondered vaguely if he should sit up on the bench too. He decided to stay where he was and made an effort to lean casually on one elbow. 'I assume this is safe,' he said. The scheduled break wasn't for another fifteen minutes.

'Batty Beattie's at a Sisters' meeting. She won't be back till twelve.'

'Beattie?' Andy grinned. 'Is that her name?'

'Beatrice. Beatrice Euphemia Meldrum. No kidding. And I'm June.'

'Andy,' he said, squeezing the hand she held out to him. 'Nice to meet you.'

Earlier, when June had shown him round the ward, there had been doctors and other staff present. She had behaved with thorough professional propriety, even a little stiffness. Nevertheless, she had managed to make it clear to Andy that she was operating from behind a carefully developed front.

'How long have you been here?' he asked her now.

'Two years. A year on Kids.' She cocked her head at him and wrinkled her nose. 'A year with Batty Beattie. It feels like ten, sometimes, but I think I've got her weighed up now.'

'She talked to me like I was a first-year student,' Andy said. 'Hit me with all the basic rules and left out the welcome.'

'She's not typical of the people here,' June assured him. 'This is a pretty good hospital – track-record-wise and staff-relations-wise. Beattie's all hung-up to hell, that's her trouble.'

'She struck me as just calcified,' Andy said. 'The way a lot of Sisters get when they should have moved on long ago – you know, set hard in her ways.'

'It's murkier than that,' June said with a slow wink. 'Sex-related. When I know you better I'll give you the dirty details.'

Andy felt the warmth spread across his face. At twenty-five he still found it difficult to stray off the track of ordinary chat with a girl – especially an attractive and provocative girl like June Reilly.

'Christ, I've shocked you.' The look on June's face was almost challenging.

'No you haven't.' Andy smiled, which always made him look more at ease than he felt in these situations. 'It's just . . .' He waved his hand vaguely, knowing his face must be scarlet by now. 'Well . . .'

'The thought of anybody like Sister Meldrum having a sex life? It's enough to make anybody blush, I suppose. I believe I did, when I found out.'

A feverish train of recollection was fast-playing through Andy's mind. In London, he'd been told, nurses were *real* ravers and *very* easygoing. He'd been told a number of lurid stories in support of the claim. And sure enough here he was, on his first working day in Walford, teetering on the brink of dirty talk with a great-looking Staffer. If he had been able to smother his shyness he might even be enjoying it.

'Have you got a girl, Andy?' Again, that challenging look. 'Somebody regular, I mean?'

Oh God, he thought. 'Well no.' His eyes wavered under her scrutiny. 'I've only just arrived in London . . .'

'Nobody back up North?'

'Not recently.' Nor ever, in any accepted sense. The possibility that he was a freak had occurred to him often. It was occurring again.

'We'll soon fix you up.' June said it as casually as if she were promising to get him a spare uniform.

To Andy it felt like a random threat. He gulped his coffee, trying to think of something that would get her off the topic. 'What's it like round here? Walford, I mean.'

'I don't know too much about it. I live in Islington. I've been in one or two of the pubs, though. They're all right, and the people are great.'

'I'm moving into a flat with some other nurses on Thursday,' he said, then hastily added, 'Male nurses. The place is on Carver Road.'

'Yucch.'

'I heard it was OK.'

'Male nurses in these parts live like pigs,' June said. 'Carver Road would need renovating to qualify as a slum. Why don't you get into mixed accommodation? There's quite a few nurses here have that arrangement. It's got to be better than an all-male set up.'

The thought terrified him. 'I'll see how it works at Carver Road. I'm taking the room on a month's trial for starters, anyway.'

The door opened and June automatically ducked her cigarette down out of sight. A smiling young Indian doctor came in.

'Oh, it's you.' June swung a smoke-trailing hand between the two men. 'Dr Malik, Staff Nurse O'Brien. He's just joined us today.'

The doctor's smile widened as he nodded to Andy. Still holding the door handle he leaned towards June. 'You're remembering Friday, I hope?'

She nodded. 'Eight sharp. I'll be there.'

Malik looked at Andy. 'Do you fancy coming, at all? We're having a party for a colleague who's going back to India.'

'Well . . .'

'Should be fun,' June said encouragingly. 'A good way of getting to know everybody, too.'

17

Andy found himself saying yes. Organising a social life here didn't appear to be any problem.

'First rate,' Malik said in his careful English. 'I'll see you both on Friday, then. Don't forget to bring a bottle.'

As Malik left June lowered her voice confidentially. 'He's a randy little sod that one, but he's got a heart of gold.'

When they had finished their coffee and were on their way back to the ward, June reassured Andy that he would soon fit in, in spite of any dark premonitions Sister Meldrum's little talk might have given him.

'With only the odd exception, everybody's out to be friendly.'

Five minutes later, as Andy leaned over the bed of a ten-year-old boy and asked him how he was coming along, the lad looked up from his comic and scowled at him.

'Piss off, Jock. I'm tryin' to read.'

One of the odd exceptions, Andy told himself as he moved on to another patient.

3

'The place is looking very smart, Mum. As usual.' Debbie stood by the fireplace, smiling at her mother as she fussed with the lunch things.

'She never stops,' Debbie's father said from his chair. 'Always goin' at it, cleanin' this, dustin' that. I reckon she's full of that stuff what keeps ants on the move.'

The Wilkins' ground-floor flat was a surprise to anyone visiting them for the first time. Not that they had many visitors. The council block, pock-marked and grimy, stood among six identical piles, designed and built at a time when architects thought they knew best how working people should live. Back in 1952 the small estate had been heralded as a pointer to the designs of the future; now, thirty years later, it looked stranger than ever, a scattering of flat-topped, brick-and-concrete oblongs, depressingly drab, standing on Walford's most cheerless boundary.

'I'm better off looking after the place than sitting there twiddling my thumbs,' Debbie's mother said, breezing off to the kitchen. Debbie grinned at her father.

Iris Wilkins had fought the gloom of her surroundings for the entire nineteen years she had lived there. Her home was a bright, tidy fortress against the immediate outside world. The bleak streets with their drifting litter, daubed walls, roaming skinny dogs and beat-up cars were reflected nowhere in the cosily furnished set of linked boxes that was the Wilkins' home.

The flat was, however, a monument to compromised

19

ideals. The spotless, rich-coloured carpets were fifty-percent nylon; washable wallpaper had been made a shade lighter by successive cleanings; stretch-covers concealed a need for a new settee and armchairs; here and there the Wonder of Woolies did service where Iris would have preferred a touch of Heal's or Habitat. There was a limit to what a working wife with an invalid husband could achieve, however strong her hopes.

'I'm whacked,' Debbie told her father. 'And there's still half the day to go yet.' Once a week she came to visit – usually, as today, at lunchtime on Monday. Today she had arrived later than usual because they were short-staffed at the bank where she worked.

'So, you've had a tough morning of it, eh?' As ever when his daughter was present, Derek Wilkins was making an effort to sound buoyant and cheerful, because he knew she worried about him. 'Can't say I've done a lot, meself.' Half-crippled by rheumatism and the disability from an accident twenty years before, Derek couldn't do much anyway, but he tried to sustain the illusion that he could make himself useful if he wanted. 'I've read the paper from front to back an' that's about the size of it.'

'I've been run off my feet,' Debbie sighed. 'And when we're busy the customers always seem to be a lot more awkward than usual.'

'How's it goin' anyway – in general that is. Makin' headway?'

'I suppose so.' Debbie had been at the bank for four years, since just after her eighteenth birthday. For the first couple of years she had felt she was little more than a skivvy; since then she had been making progress, but at times it seemed woefully slow. 'If I was a man, I'd get on a lot faster.'

Derek tut-tutted, as if he were hearing the complaint for the first time. 'Discrimination, eh? I'd have thought Women's Lib would have changed all that.'

Debbie shook her head. 'They haven't made a mark on banking. Women really have to prove themselves before they get promotion. And even then it's slow-motion stuff – none of the big leaps some of the men make.'

'Don't fret, love. I'm sure you'll show 'em all, one of these days.'

Debbie looked at her father hunched in his chair, seeing the pain-lined eyes, the delicate, always semi-sad mouth. 'I'm determined enough, Dad.'

'Course you are. You're a Wilkins.'

Iris came back from the kitchen with a covered Pyrex dish. 'Come and get it then, while it's hot.'

Debbie helped her father out of his chair as Iris began scooping shepherd's pie on to the plates set out on the small dining table.

'I've told you not to make anything special when I come round, Mum.'

'It's not anything special.'

Debbie knew differently. Usually lunch here was sandwiches and a cup of tea. Evening meals were often just as frugal. Severe economies on food and clothing were essential, since rent and fuel bills took a major chunk out of Iris's wages and Derek's disability pension. Monday lunch, Debbie suspected, was probably the culinary high spot of the week.

When they had eaten and Derek had gone back to the relative comfort of his fireside chair, Debbie and her mother had their customary chat over a cup of instant.

'I've taken on another little job,' Iris eventually announced. Her brows moved closer at once, as if to

21

ward off Debbie's predictable response. 'Just an hour in the evenings . . .'

'Oh, Mum. You work evenings as it is . . .'

'Well beggars can't be choosers. Not that we're beggars, of course, but every little helps.'

'Even so. How many jobs have you got already? Three?'

'Four,' Iris mumbled. 'They're all light work.'

'Individually. Add them together and they're hard work.' Debbie shook her head at her mother. 'Didn't you go round to the Social Security like I told you? They've got schemes to help, you know. You only have to ask.'

'Beg, more likely.'

The dread spectre of official help was something Iris would never countenance. She had always coped on her own. That way she held on to her dignity. That way she maintained her unique local status as someone who relied on the State for practically nothing. Self-support meant a great deal to Iris Wilkins, even if it had aged her prematurely.

'Social Security's all right for people that don't have any pride, Debbie.'

'Now that's not fair, Mum. Some people can't help themselves, remember.'

'Some,' Iris said grudgingly. 'Not as many as make out they can't. Half of them round here would starve sooner than help themselves. But they don't have to starve *or* work, do they? They can go down to the DHSS with their begging bowls.'

Debbie decided not to pursue the argument. It would get her nowhere. There was so much tied up with her mother's attitude that had to remain unspoken. Like the small snobberies she permitted herself – ignoring most of her neighbours, talking differently from them, making

22

sure top-quality biscuit-wrappers, magazines and news-papers – picked up on her cleaning jobs – were frequently seen sticking out of her dustbin. A woman of that calibre, with a daughter who worked in a bank no less, wouldn't be caught dead at the Supplementary Benefits window.

'What kind of a wild weekend did you have?' Derek asked. He asked that every Monday.

Debbie smiled across at him. 'The usual. Friday night swotting. Saturday in bed till ten, then a few hours tidying up the place.' Debbie lived in a large flat near her bank in Wandsworth. She shared the place with two other women and three men. 'At night me and the girls went to a wine bar and had a Chinese meal afterwards. Most of Sunday I just lay around, reading the papers and watching telly, then I did some more swotting and went to bed. End of wild weekend.'

'They sound like a nice bunch, your flatmates,' Iris said. 'The men – they're in business too, is that right?'

'One's in banking, one's in television rentals, one's an insurance assessor.' Debbie had told her mother that before, but she knew the litany reassured her. To Iris's way of thinking, men who were in business were much less likely to take liberties than men who weren't. She had no real idea if her daughter's virginity was still intact – which it was – but she had the soothing certainty that Debbie always moved in the kind of circles where it was least likely to be lost.

'Oh gosh, look at the time.'

Debbie swallowed her coffee and stood up, smoothing the pleats of her skirt. She saw her father's mouth grow a little sadder. These visits were so brief, she thought, too brief. They never managed to get a decent conversation going before it was time for her to get back to the bank. But no other arrangement was possible. Her mother

23

worked mornings and afternoons at weekends, and her father always had to go to bed early.

As she pulled on her jacket she bent and kissed Derek's cheek. 'Take care now, Dad. Remember to take your medicine.'

'Righto.' Derek squeezed her hand. 'See you next week, love.' His eyes followed her proudly to the door, where Iris stood ready to see her out.

In the tiny hallway the women embraced fleetingly by the picture of The Boy With the Tear. Debbie promised to come over earlier next week and Iris promised to take things easy. The front door opened and closed and Debbie went hurrying along the windy April street.

One of the Wilkins' neighbours, a fat woman with a face that looked as if it had recently been boiled, nudged her equally obese companion as the pretty, smartly dressed blonde girl walked past them.

'There goes Miss Hoity-Toity.'

'Who's she?'

'Old Wilkins' daughter.'

The companion glanced back. She nodded admiringly. 'Good-looking girl, mind you.'

'They brung her up like she was precious china. Never let her out with the other kids. Made her into a right stuck-up little madam.'

'Mm,' the companion mused. 'Now you mention it, it does look like butter wouldn't melt in her mouth.'

'Nor anywhere else.'

As Debbie approached the bus stop she was thinking about her dad – her *poor* dad, as he always was in her mind – shut up in there all day with his pain, and about her mother, stooped, ageing, honed-down by work and worry. Every Monday the same thoughts beset her, filling her with uneasiness and a moping guilt. But what could she do? They wouldn't accept money from her, after all. They wouldn't have her living with them, either. What *could* she do?

Today, though, the brooding and the sad, sentimental images didn't linger. She had a problem. It had overshadowed her all weekend. As she boarded her bus all thought of her parents fled as she returned to some fretting on her own account.

She got back to the bank three minutes late. Fortunately everybody was too busy to take any notice. Debbie put away her jacket and took up her position at the till.

The first customer was well known to her. Miss Trent, the retired English and needlework teacher who had cataracts and was never sure which cashier she was dealing with. She had come to pay in the usual wad of miscounted, unsorted notes. The cash was, incredibly, the proceeds of private tuition. Miss Trent had never specified whether it was English or needlework she taught privately, though Debbie believed English was the least unlikely. How, though, did she check her students' work? To sign a paying-in slip, the old lady had to put her face very close to the paper, and even then she sometimes missed.

'I make it thirty-one pounds altogether, Miss Trent.'

The woman peered at the glass screen. 'Oh my. Are you sure?'

'Absolutely sure.'

'Someone must have overpaid me. It should only be twenty-eight.'

'Perhaps you mixed up some other money with it,' Debbie suggested.

Miss Trent was thinking. 'Lord!' she said suddenly. She looked shocked. 'Three pounds over. I think I know what it is.' She got out her antique purse and undid the catch. After fumbling around in a side pocket for a minute, she shook her head sadly. 'Poor man. What must he think?'

'Sorry?'

'The milkman. I owed him two weeks' money. Three pounds. I left it out for him yesterday. Oh my.'

Debbie didn't understand. 'If you left it out for him – '

'They've gone from my purse, you see. I keep things in separate compartments, so I won't get muddled. But I must have made a mistake this time.'

'What's gone from your purse?'

'Three tickets for the Baptist Church raffle. Oh Lord.'

When Miss Trent had been sorted out and dispatched into the bewildering world outside, an impatient-looking man stepped forward. He held up the fingers of one hand. Debbie stared at them politely.

'Five minutes I've been waiting,' he snapped.

'I'm sorry, sir. We're very busy today.'

'I don't pay extortionate bank charges to have my time wasted hanging about in here, you know.'

'I'm very sorry.' Debbie waited for him to state his business, but he wasn't ready to do that yet.

'I mean look at the time of day, and there's only three of you on the tills. What the hell are all those others doing? Hmm? Walking about with bits of paper in their hands, skiving off while customers are left dangling – '

'I've said I'm sorry, sir. I'm afraid there was nothing I could do about the delay.'

'It's a flaming scandal.'

Debbie swallowed hard, clinging tightly to her courteous expression. 'How can I help you, sir?'

He blinked at her a couple of times before the question sank in. 'It's my cash-dispenser card. My wife's, actually. Your machine's kept it.'

'Did the machine indicate why?'

He shrugged, making light of his error in advance. 'I didn't key in the right number. I must have memorized it wrong.'

Debbie asked him, in her most careful voice, what he wanted her to do.

'Give me the bloody thing back, that's what.'

'Is your wife a customer at this branch?'

He shook his head. 'No, she isn't. Why?'

'Because the card can only be returned by the branch where it originated.'

The man put his face close to the screen and glared at her. 'Listen, it's bad enough I've been kept waiting so long, without you throwing in all this bureaucratic guff – '

'I'm very sorry, but we can't return cards that weren't issued by our branch.' Before he could say any more, Debbie added, 'And even if it had come from this branch, we wouldn't be able to give it to you.'

'What?' He looked thunderstruck.

'You don't have the right to use the card, sir. It's your wife's.'

The tirade that followed required the stern handling of the Assistant Manager, who marched the man off into a private room to frighten him with the legal position, freeing Debbie to attend to the rest of her customers.

So far, she was thinking, it was a pretty normal afternoon on the till. Then she looked up and saw Personal Problem Number One staring at her through the glass. Although she knew he would turn up, she had been silently praying he wouldn't.

'Hello, Debbie.'

'Good afternoon, Mr Borrowfield,' she said curtly.

He gave her his winner's smile. The teeth were white and even, set within a tanned face with regular features

27

topped by thick, impeccably trimmed brown hair. He stood as if a camera was trained on him, smiling, an elbow on the edge of the counter.

'Can I help you?'

'You know you can.'

The suit, like the rest of his appearance, was decidedly up-market. It was incredible, Debbie thought, that somebody who looked so great could be such a repulsive slob.

'I'm rather busy at the moment, and there are other people waiting . . .'

'Just say yes,' he drawled, 'then tell me the time and place, and I'll leave you to get on.'

The man's consummate confidence in his charm was unnerving. His persistence, nearly a week old by now, had passed the unnerving stage. In spite of his benign smile, his soft voice and his manicured grace, Colin Borrowfield had begun to scare Debbie. Badly.

'I'm sure you've got the wrong idea about me, Debbie,' he said as she stared at him. 'Why the stiff face?' He lowered his voice; 'Suspenders too tight, are they?'

It had started two weeks before. Borrowfield, a property dealer and a valued customer of the branch, had accosted Debbie on the street. His car drew up right beside her, he stepped out and invited her to dinner. Debbie recalled that his confidence at that point had been merely disarming.

Even though she had always found the man attractive, Debbie declined. She thought it wasn't proper to accept an invitation so abruptly delivered, without preamble. And something else was wrong, though she couldn't quite define it. At that point Borrowfield hadn't persisted. He simply suggested she think it over, then he got back in his shiny Porsche and drove away.

But the same thing happened two days after. Then

again the day after that. When Debbie still refused to go out with him, Borrowfield began coming into the banking hall with his offer of dinner and the added enticement, by then, of 'somewhere nice afterwards'.

He had been coming in every day since the previous Monday, giving Debbie the weekend free to magnify her nervousness and annoyance into fear. The thing that was wrong, the thing she hadn't been able to define at first, was clear enough to her now. It was the way Borrowfield looked at her. His eyes signalled raw, frightening, compulsive lust. The other girls at the flat would have laughed themselves silly if she'd told them that, but it was true. Some of the things Borrowfield had started saying backed up Debbie's certainty. It wasn't at all like being fancied. There was nothing even remotely decent in the feverish ambition she saw behind those cool brown eyes.

'So what do you say?' He was still gazing at her, still smiling.

'Please . . .' Debbie felt herself losing control. She had no power, she thought, to repulse him. It was like finding herself defenceless in the face of some dire curse. 'You mustn't keep this up. I'm – '

'Just say yes, Debbie. I told you already.'

She turned from the till suddenly and stamped off towards the cloakroom. 'Take over for me please, Betty,' she managed to say as she swept past a junior clerk. In the cloakroom she locked herself in a stall and began to cry.

4

On Wednesday Andy O'Brien was taken to the Baby Room adjacent to Maternity. The man who took him was Dr Malcolm Norris, a Consultant Paediatrician who had already impressed Andy with his sharp talent for diagnosis and his warm, understanding way with the children on the ward.

As they walked along the echoing corridor towards Maternity the doctor chatted easily. He was probably no more than ten years older than Andy; his style made him seem even younger.

'Not too many men specialize in children's nursing,' Norris said. 'Did you feel it was a vocation?'

Andy shook his head. 'It was force of circumstances, Doctor. After I'd qualified in general nursing there was an employment problem. My alternative to the dole was an eighteen-month specialist course at the Royal Hospital for Sick Children in Glasgow. After I'd completed that I applied for a few positions and finally landed the job here.'

'Would you rather be doing something else?'

As with all serious questions, Andy gave it careful consideration before he answered. 'A year ago I thought so, yes. But not now.'

Norris smiled. The reply obviously pleased him. 'There's something about paediatrics, isn't there? The child evolving to adulthood – it's a very special creature. With amazingly special clinical problems. You virtually have to re-think and adapt every medical concept you learned in your training. I've known times when – ' He stopped abruptly and smiled again, rather apologetically. 'I start rambling on about it at the drop of an opportunity.'

'So do I,' Andy confessed.

When they reached the Baby Room they took masks from a sterile container behind the door and put them on. They moved into the warm, bright-lit bay with its rows of white-and-green cots. Three nurses, masked and gowned, patrolled the short aisles like warders.

'The reason I brought you here,' Norris told Andy, 'is because I believe we see clinical trends develop in this place. I think senior nurses should be conscious of future patterns on the children's ward.'

They stopped by a cot where Andy had already seen a nurse pause and frown at the infant lying there.

'This is Dorothy,' Dr Norris said. 'She's not quite four days old.'

The child was lying on a stiffish white mattress no bigger than a bed pillow. Her weight was charted at four pounds ten ounces. Her appearance was normal – thin arms and legs with ill-fitting skin, disproportionately large head, hands clenched into miraculously small fists. Dorothy's behaviour, however, was far from normal. She twitched, shuddered, gulped air every few seconds. She also appeared to be sweating.

'Her other symptoms,' Norris said after a moment, 'are fits of extreme irritability, diarrhoea and vomiting.' He looked at Andy. 'What do you make of it?'

Andy stared at the baby. 'I've no idea. Maybe it could be hypoglycaemia . . .' He looked at the baby again and shook his head. 'No. She's got too many contradictory symptoms for that.' He leaned closer as the child arched its back and shivered. Her eyes opened, rolled around then clamped shut again. She grunted, twice; it was a sound that would have surprised him less if it had come from an animal. Andy straightened and faced Dr Norris. 'Apart from making a guess at birth trauma, I can't imagine what this is.'

'Dorothy's mother is a junkie,' Norris said. 'The child, God help her, is suffering from drug withdrawal.'

'Heavens.' Andy looked at the child again. 'What drug? Heroin?'

'Methadone,' Norris said. 'It's a bit of an irony. The mother switched to the methadone as an alternative to heroin. Technically it's not so harmful, as you know. But a baby's withdrawal symptoms are always worse with methadone.'

Andy watched the little creature twitch and jitter the way he had seen grown addicts do in Glasgow. 'Didn't she know she'd be passing the drug on to the baby?'

'The mother is seventeen. She's a prostitute and a long-term drug abuser. On top of that she's as thick as a navvy's sandwich. Subtle possibilities such as drug transference would never enter her skull.'

'Do you get many of these?'

Norris sighed behind his mask. 'I'm afraid we do. Dorothy's the fifth this year. Three of the others weren't quite so bad as this, one was worse.'

Dr Norris went on to outline the treatment Dorothy would receive if her symptoms got any worse. She would be given diluted laudanum, the old-fashioned name for tincture of opium. In effect, one form of addiction would be used to combat the other. It was the only way to still the infant and save her from the nightmare process of long-term methadone withdrawal. Afterwards, of course, she would have to be weaned slowly away from the opium.

'The child who was worse than this one died. His heart

couldn't take the hammering from his nervous system.' Norris touched Andy's elbow and indicated a cot further along the line. 'In case you think Dorothy's the worst we have to deal with at present . . .'

They moved to the other cot. 'This is Gregory. He's two weeks old.'

Andy looked in the cot. He was accustomed to fearful sights, but he was shocked by what he saw lying there. The baby's arms and legs were flexed and taut, as if its joints had shrunk. There appeared to be only one crease in the palm of each hand. But it was the head that was truly shocking. It was unbelievably small. Andy had never seen a living head that small, even on an infant with half the body-size of this one. The child also had a gaping harelip and a cleft palate. The eyes were no larger than peas and there were several tiny slits in the eyelids.

'That's an extreme case,' Dr Norris said, 'though not a terribly rare one.'

Andy looked at him questioningly.

'It's FAS – Foetal Alcohol Syndrome. The mother's an alcoholic. In spite of a lot of vigilance by her doctor, her husband and other members of her family, she managed to drink heavily right through her pregnancy.'

'I've seen a few cases of FAS,' Andy murmured. 'Nothing as bad as this, though.' He glanced down at the silent, staring child. 'What are his chances?'

'Well, if you'll add, to what you can see, a malformed brain and a heart that's beginning to display signs of malfunction, I think you can guess.'

Andy could guess, all right. If the baby didn't die, it would grow into a grotesque, severely handicapped vegetable.

'Gregory's the third case of this kind I've seen here in

two years.' Norris sighed again. 'Come on, it gets depressing after a while.'

They removed their masks in the ante-room and went to the canteen, where Dr Norris bought them both coffee. 'Don't worry about Sister Meldrum,' he told Andy as they took their cups to a table. 'As far as she's concerned, this is a period of intensive-advanced-tuition time you're clocking up.' He winked as he sat down. 'Jargon really impresses her.'

They talked for a few minutes about the two children in the Baby Room. After a while Dr Norris asked Andy for a personal opinion; why did he think cases like those were on the increase? Andy tried to oblige.

'I suppose it's a loss of moral anchoring,' he said. 'If more and more kids are being born like that, it can only mean there are fewer and fewer moral anchors among the young adult population.' Andy thought that sounded resonably profound.

'But why?' Norris asked. 'Why the loss of moral anchorage?'

Andy frowned. 'Religion doesn't have the hold it once did . . .'

'Why?'

The frown deepened. 'Well. People are more enlightened, I suppose, or more inquisitive. They seek out their own answers . . .'

Norris smiled faintly. 'Enlightenment and a thirst for knowledge, I've found, have a tendency to tighten the moral outlook.'

Andy wondered if he was being played with. Perhaps Norris wasn't the nice guy he had appeared to be. Maybe he was having a bit of intellectual fun at Andy's expense.

'What do *you* reckon then?' Andy asked sharply, forgetting matters of rank and protocol.

Norris sipped his coffee slowly and put down the cup. 'I think a lot of people's creative and survival drives are turning to shit. They're into destruction on a big scale.'

Andy hesitated, then decided to risk it. 'Why?' he demanded.

'I can give you two answers,' Norris said. 'Because our masters have no compassion. That's one of the reasons that have been put forward. We exist in a climate of jackbooted indifference to the spiritual frailty at the centre of every one of us. Government policy, in short, is screwing up a lot of our weaker brethren.'

'Do you believe that?' Andy asked.

'Do you?'

'I don't know. I'd have to think about it.'

'Then think about the other reason while you're at it. Society's grown decadent through an overdose of free- dom. Like the Roman Empire – there's widespread permissiveness, easy access to just about anything, no real need any more. Without hardship we perish.' Norris tilted his head. 'How does that one strike you?'

Andy shrugged. 'Same as the other one. I don't know, it needs a bit of thought. Do you believe either reason yourself.'

'I'm inclined towards the first one,' Norris murmured. 'I suspect it's not the fault of the people. It's the fault of the despair they've been handed in place of their hope and their dignity. Here endeth the lesson.' He picked up his cup and drained it.

Andy did the same and they stood up. As they went to the door Dr Norris said, 'Just remember, you'll be seeing more of the Dorothys and Gregorys. More battered kids, too, more neglected ones.' He shook his head. 'In other departments they'll be handling more drunks, more junk- ies, more attempted suicides.'

'And there's nothing we can do, apart from containing the situation.'

'That's true,' Norris said. 'But containment's important. Vital. And the more compassion we hand out, the better we'll do our job.'

Back in the ward, June Reilly asked Andy how his little pep-session with the Consultant had gone.

'You knew that's what it was, did you?'

'Sure. He gave me one, too. A crash-course in sociology.'

Andy began setting out the medication on the drug trolley. 'Tell me something – is Dr Norris a Socialist? I'm a bit naïve about politics and political types, but I get the feeling . . .'

'He's nothing you can hang a label on,' June assured him. 'He's just concerned. He likes people and he's dead sensitive about things like unemployment and redundancy and all kinds of social injustice. He believes we need to be aware of all that so we can do our jobs better.'

Andy nodded. 'Compassion, he said. He seems to believe a lot of baddies aren't responsible for their actions.' He looked at June. 'That *sounds* kind of Socialist to me.'

June shook her head. 'You know what Dr Norris said when one of his uppity housemen asked him his opinion about some political thing or other?'

'What?'

'He said all political answers are wrong.'

Andy was still musing over that five minutes later when Sister Meldrum materialized at his side. She was carrying a clipboard. For a moment he thought she might be doing a time-and-motion study on him.

'You indulge in a lot of sport, don't you?' she said. She made it sound like a perversion.

'A fair amount, Sister. Football, squash, a bit of running . . .'

'Right. I'm putting your name down.' She began writing on the paper on the board.

'For what?'

'A sports day.' She finished writing his name and looked up with the shadow of a scowl. 'I don't particularly hold with it, but I'm required to supply the names of any of my staff who have proficiency in sport.'

'What kind of sports day?' Andy heard the aggressive edge that had entered his voice and decided not to hamper it. He might be at Sister Meldrum's service but he wasn't her doormat. 'I like to be asked about that kind of thing and make my own mind up.'

Oddly, she seemed to take it well. She showed no more than impatience as she explained. 'Every year a team assembled from East London hospitals competes with another team drawn from the staff of some bank or other. It's next month. You'll get the full details later. All right?'

Andy thought about it. It sounded fine. 'Yes, I suppose it's all right, Sister. I'll give it a go.'

'I've got your name down anyway,' Sister pointed out as she turned and swept away.

Later, wheeling the drug trolley towards the bed of Jackie Loughton, Andy's mind drifted back to what Dr Norris had said. Jackie was nine and he was frightened of practically everything that moved. As Andy approached the boy slid down under the covers until all that showed was the top of his tousled head.

'I've got your medicine here, Jackie.'

The little hummock of blanket didn't move.

'It's the red stuff that tastes like cherries.' Carefully, Andy reached out and uncovered the boy's face. Big

37

dark eyes stared back at him. The bruised lips were shut tight. 'Tell you what,' Andy murmured, 'I'll take some of it, if you will.' He glanced fearfully over his shoulder. 'If you don't have any, Sister's going to take one of my badges off me.' He touched the Sick Children's Nursing shield on his chest. 'This one.' He saw a glimmer of curiosity break through the lad's caution. 'I'll sit here and maybe we can have a chat until you're ready for the medicine.'

He drew up a child-size chair and perched on it, making it creak. It would be hard to have compassion for both this boy *and* the man who battered him. Jackie had been beaten by his drunken father; his mother, coming home and finding the boy semi-conscious, had summoned the police and an ambulance. When Jackie had been brought to the hospital, five days ago, he had been found to have concussion, a broken rib, a dislocated shoulder and severe general bruising.

'Would you like to look at the badge Sister's after?' Andy unhooked it and offered it to Jackie. 'Mind the pin.' He held it out until his arm ached. Finally one small hand reached from the blankets and took the badge. The child held it close to himself, examining it shyly.

Compassion, Andy thought. Until now he assumed he'd plenty of it, certainly enough for the kind of job he did. But now he was being told – or believed he was being told – that he should extend the range of his compassion to take in the kind of swine he would sooner go five rounds with. It would take some doing. He was seriously prepared to think over what the Consultant had said, though. He had a lot of respect for the man. Nobody that good at his job, that *concerned*, could get things entirely wrong.

Jackie offered back the badge. Andy took it and leaned closer to the bed.

'Do you know anything about sports, Jackie?' he asked confidentially. 'I need somebody to help me out. Sister's told me I've got to go in an egg-and-spoon race or something. She says if I don't, she'll take my other badge off me, too.'

For the first time since he arrived in the ward, Jackie Loughton smiled.

5

The place smelled faintly of trapped air and old vegetables. Beside the pile of newspapers and magazines in the hall a grey cat sat licking its rump. Geoff Mercer, looking fairly laid-back in his bleached jeans and striped rugby shirt, strode across to the closed door beside the bathroom and twisted the handle. The door didn't budge.

'Flaming thing.'

He put his shoulder to the door's edge and jerked. It flew open suddenly, revealing the bare-walled bedroom beyond.

'There you go, squire.' He grinned and tossed back a lank strand of fair hair. 'What do you think?'

Andy had been warned that it was unwise to take any accommodation in Walford without seeing it first, but it looked like he'd been lucky here. He walked into the room and put down his bags by the single bed.

'Not bad,' he murmured.

'My room's not as big as this,' Geoff said encouragingly, not sure how to take Andy's poker-faced response. 'Not as light, either. I was going to move in here when Bernie left, but I've got used to my gloomy little pothole. I decided to stay put.'

'I like it,' Andy said. 'It's just the job.' What he liked was the blandness of the ten-by-twelve enclosure. It was thoroughly neutral. There was nobody's mark on it, no character or atmosphere that he might have to subdue before he could settle in. 'You won't mind if I tart it up a bit?'

'Do what you like,' Geoff said. Although the lease was his, he had emphasized that he didn't want to be looked upon as a landlord. 'Put in a barbecue. Grow cannabis in the window box. Play Status Quo albums all day – anything at all. You're going to have to put up with our foibles, after all.'

Andy nodded, seeing just the spot to hang his Adidas sports calendar. 'I'm going to like it here.'

The air of democracy was reinforced a few minutes later when the other occupant, Ralph Dixon, came clanging in through the front door with an armful of canned food, cereal boxes and a six-pack of lager.

'Evening, all,' he yelled, taking his load into the kitchen and dumping it noisily on the table. 'Beer-up, if anybody's interested.'

Andy and Geoff joined him. Ralph had already ripped open two cans and was carefully filling a glass with the manner of an affable barman. He looked up at Andy, who towered a good eight inches above him. 'I know it's more macho to drink it out of the can,' he said, 'but I'm always scared somebody gets his tongue sliced off on the edge of the hole.'

They toasted the future of their domestic trinity. After a top-up they sat down around the table. Ralph, a surgical Staff Nurse with an uncanny resemblance to the young Adam Faith, gave Andy a speedy rundown of their relationship with their neighbours in the flat upstairs and in the adjacent buildings.

'They're pretty suspicious of us. You know how it is with people – especially the basic types round here with their one inch of forehead and the slow blink-rate. They need to get you pigeon-holed pretty smartish, and with us it's no problem. Male nurses, living together. We've got to be bent. Stands to reason.'

'Against all the evidence,' Geoff Mercer murmured, smiling. 'There's more crumpet goes in and out that front door than you could shake a gross of Durex at, but it doesn't change the general local opinion. At best we're odd. Real men just don't do women's work, do they?'

Andy had learned to live with the stigma long ago. In one Glasgow pub he had been whisperingly nicknamed The Laddie With the Lamp, to the accompaniment of furtive limp-wristed gestures as he entered the bar. He finally cancelled all misunderstandings about his manhood by grabbing one of the sniggerers and threatening to make him eat the landlord's whippet – whole.

'I suppose it's going to aggravate matters, you being another adonis type,' Ralph grunted to Andy. 'If we were all as runty as me we'd have better street credibility.' He swallowed some lager and sighed. 'Still. It's cheap, living round here.'

Within an hour, the air of welcome had blended smoothly to an atmosphere that resembled long-standing communal harmony. When all the lager had been consumed Andy unpacked, giving the bedroom the stamp of his individual untidiness. Meanwhile Geoff threw together a supper of scrambled eggs and toast for the three of them, while Ralph spent ten minutes on the 'phone, trying to knock a private vendor down to a reasonable price for a 1976 Allegro.

After their meal they lolled in the sitting room, half watching Top of the Pops on a colour set with a defect that rendered one corner of the picture bright pink.

'I don't know why I sit through all this, week in and week out,' Geoff said. Unlike the other two, he had a clinic job which left him free every evening; he was relied upon by Ralph to keep him up to date on programmes he missed. 'This show's like panning for gold – spotting the odd bright glint in heap after heap of shit.'

Andy was preoccupied with his surroundings. The room was high-ceilinged and rather draughty, with ancient heavy curtains, ruptured armchairs and a carpet that was worn down to canvas in places. It pleased Andy as much as his bedroom. It was stable, neutral and solid; he had the feeling that no matter what you did in there, you couldn't do the place any harm.

Bonnie Tyler had been holding Ralph's attention, but when Spandau Ballet came on he yawned and glanced across at Andy. 'Do you reckon you'll settle in all right? Not just here I mean – at the hospital, in London itself.'

Andy was glad of an opportunity to explain. It got his history out of the way quickly. As a foster child, he said, homesickness had long since ceased to be a problem. Having always been the odd one out, he had nevertheless always felt that he belonged, wherever he found himself.

'I've been a member of quite a few families. Always a welcome member, too. I've had a few mums and dads, loads of brothers and sisters, and I'm used to the idea of interchangeable environments. I'm conditioned to fit in.'

'Ironical, isn't it?' Geoff muttered, his eyes still on the television set. 'Because you belonged to nobody, you were treated like you belonged to everybody.'

Andy nodded. 'I was never spoiled or pampered when I was a kid, either. I always had to pull my weight. That helped me to feel independent.'

'Ever wondered about where you came from?' Ralph asked him.

'If I ever did wonder, I've forgotten. I'm not curious to know who my real parents were. I don't even know if I'm really Scottish.'

Geoff nodded, appearing to approve of Andy's detachment and adaptability. 'No ties then, eh?'

Andy shrugged. 'I daresay I'll develop them, when the time's right.' The vague notion of a wife and children, somewhere in the future, was the only idea of attachment he had ever entertained. He had no confidence that the family would ever materialize, though.

'If you want to take on some strong ties,' Ralph said, 'the real heavy, guilt-ridden kind, I'll be happy to pass on some of mine.'

The television was forgotten as they rearranged themselves to discuss Ralph's domination by his mother, plus the bad conscience he had about not following his father into engineering, plus the squirmy sense of betrayal he suffered because he wouldn't commit himself fully to his current girlfriend.

At that point – inevitably, Andy thought – the talk turned sharply from the difficulty of relationships to the addictive qualities of sex.

'It's the only thing most people haven't lost faith in,' Geoff said airily. 'That's why they're always at it.'

'Yeah.' Ralph gazed thoughtfully across the room. 'If it really did make you go blind, somebody would be making millions out of white sticks.' He grinned. 'There'd be a chronic shortage of Labradors and Alsations, too.'

Behind his head-nodding, wide-grinning cover, Andy was suffering the old awkwardness that took him every time sex went under the spotlight. It was bad enough to feel like a fraud, like somebody with fake credentials, but it was even worse to know that some day he might get caught. He only had to hear the word 'virgin' to get a crawly feeling that somebody was going to aim it at *him* and demand that he prove them wrong.

Geoff looked at him. In the handsome, confident

features Andy saw a hint of the challenge he'd detected in June Reilly. 'I don't suppose you've been here long enough to try out the local talent, have you?'

Andy shook his head. 'I've scarcely got my bearings.'

'It won't take you long,' Ralph promised him. 'A couple of weeks of the local wine-bar society and you'll be going at it like a rat up a drainpipe.'

'We might get a party organized,' Geoff suggested. 'Just a little gathering to smooth your path. It'll have to wait till pay day, though.'

Andy told them he'd already been invited to a party. 'Tomorrow, as a matter of fact. It's for some doctor that's going back to India.'

Geoff and Ralph made sour faces at him.

'Dr Gupta's do,' Geoff said. 'It'll be a washout, mate. At those affairs, male nurses are about as welcome as Mary Whitehouse at a Motorhead concert.'

'Oh.' Andy was surprised. 'June Reilly seemed to think I'd enjoy myself . . .'

'June's a classic example of the problem,' Ralph said. 'She's strictly a doctor's dolly. At those parties all the girls are. Everybody'll be nice to you all right, and I daresay you could have a fair amount of fun, so long as you don't try to pull a woman for yourself.'

'Dead right,' Geoff said. 'You'll soon get the elbow if you try any of that.'

Andy had never been to any doctors' parties in Scotland, but he had heard similar stories. He would have thought it would be different here in enlightened, liberal old London.

'Oh well,' he murmured. 'I'll just try to make the best of it.' On balance, he was now looking forward to the party a shade more than he had been before. If he didn't make a play for a girl, it would just be assumed he was sticking to the rules. As he reflected on that, his mind shot him a question it had been asking a lot recently: *So WHEN are you going to make the effort?*

Geoff tapped the face of his watch. 'Drinkie-pooh time.'

'I'm seeing Edna,' Ralph said, a little glumly.

Geoff looked enquiringly at Andy. 'Coming? I'll introduce you to the crowd and get you some kind of credit-rating with the guv'nor.'

'Sounds good to me,' Andy said.

'Make sure he meets Deirdre,' Ralph said as Geoff and Andy stood up.

'Not on his first night,' Geoff said. 'That'd be like putting a novice in the bullring with a rhino.' He smiled at Andy. 'No reflection on you, mate – it's just that Deirdre's a bit different. Heavily into sexual harassment, especially if you're over five-foot eight. We'll stick with the quieter end of the gang, for tonight anyway.'

Yes, Andy thought fervently, let's just do that.

That Thursday evening Debbie stayed late at the bank to help with a public relations exercise. Twenty young people about to leave school were shown round and introduced to the mechanics of banking, from the taking and issuing of cash, to the more complex procedures like foreign business transactions and securities. Senior staff did all the talking and demonstrating; Debbie and another couple of girls handed out coffee and biscuits and answered occasional questions about their jobs.

Ordinarily, Debbie would have found this a bore. Tonight, though, she was prepared to see it as a necessary part of her rôle in the bank. For three days, in fact, she had been growing more and more ready to apply herself at full stretch, however mundane or trivial the task on hand. She had reached a point where she felt that nothing, or almost nothing, was too much trouble. She was building a career, after all. To do that properly, she should learn and exercise thorough commitment.

Deep down she knew what it was really all about. She was still sailing on a tide of purest, sheerest relief. Since her little breakdown on Monday, Colin Borrowfield hadn't been in the bank. There had been no sign of him, not even on Wednesday morning when he normally brought in the takings from the charity raffle at his businessmen's circle. Somebody else had brought in the money. Borrowfield had got the message, Debbie decided. He had finally realized there was no point in pursuing her. The removal of that overload from her nervous system had put new vigour in her.

Towards the end of the evening, when the young visitors were being shown a promotional video in the computer room, Debbie sat down at the counter with the leaflets she had received through the post that morning. They were educational information sheets, pointers to the way up in her profession.

Buoyant as she felt, the next set of examinations looked pretty daunting. In the space of a year she would need to gain a sound understanding of the law relating to banking. As if that wasn't enough, she would have to learn a great deal about monetary economics and accountancy, too. And that was far from being the end of the matter. In many respects it was only a beginning, a door that opened on to others.

She read the papers over carefully, conscious all the time of the image she held precious, the vision of herself in management. It was the holiest thing in her life, something rather too big, Debbie felt, to be simply called ambition. It meant security and independence, it meant she could exercise authority and mature judgement. Most glorious of all, a management position would mean she could run her own life precisely the way she wanted.

Her eyes wandered over the subjects that lay even further ahead, perhaps two or three years away, each one a hurdle that couldn't be side-stepped if she was to succeed. They read like a list of the most solemn duties – Nature of Management, Advanced Banking Law, Investment, Finance of International Trade . . .

'Any biscuits left?'

Debbie looked up and saw Trudie, a junior who had been with the bank for less than a year. 'There's a plate over there,' Debbie said.

'Ta. I'm starved.'

Trudie went off with Debbie's gaze trailing her. She knew there was something not quite fair in the way she drew comfort from girls like that, but she couldn't help herself. The kid was always in trouble, always being told off for being late, for making silly mistakes, for conducting herself badly with customers. Trudie was a salutary warning. She was a living catalogue of what it took to be a failure in this business.

Returning her attention to the pamphlets, Debbie warned herself that she was sliding into smugness. Just because she had been a good girl all along, a fastidious little employee with a sound branch record and good examination results – that didn't mean she'd grown immune to failure. There were still all those hurdles to clear.

On the way home she stopped at a shop on the corner and looked at some dresses. More and more, she tended to buy clothes that mirrored the person she wanted to become, rather than the girl she currently was. Slightly old-fashioned, that was what one of the girls at the flat had been candid enough to call Debbie's line in party wear. Even her tennis gear had a lot of modesty built-in, or so the same girl had told her. If anything, Debbie believed she favoured the chic in clothing, with just a touch of professional sobriety. There was a dress right in the centre of the window that looked like it fitted the formula.

The focus of her gaze switched suddenly as she saw a familiar, frightening reflection in the glass. Across the road, a lovingly-waxed red Porsche had drawn up. In the dimness of the reflection she couldn't see the driver. She didn't have to.

'God,' she heard herself moan. She began moving sideways, keeping her face to the window. The car was still sitting there. Debbie counted slowly to ten, then turned sharply, prepared to make a run for it if she had to.

The car took off with a squeal of rubber as she reached the edge of the pavement. Debbie's heart thudded as she teetered, wondering if she could make it into the road before he drew up at the kerb. She took four quick steps forward then froze as the car growled towards her.

'Oh no, God please – '

It went past. She saw an elderly, detached-looking man at the wheel. And it was a Saab. A brown one.

Debbie got to the other side of the road and stopped, her hand clinging to a lamp post. She was shaking.

'Debs – you all right?'

It was Trudie again. She had left the bank a couple of minutes after Debbie.

'Yes, I'm fine.' Debbie took a deep breath, feeling foolish now.

'You look like you seen a ghost.'

'I'm all right, Trudie. Just felt a bit funny for a minute, that's all.'

After a further moment's inspection of Debbie's ashen face, Trudie shrugged. 'Well, so long as you're OK . . .'

'Yes. Thanks, Trudie.'

'See you tomorrow, then. Tara.'

The girl trotted away. Debbie remained where she was, panting softly, telling herself what an idiot she was, trying to conjure back that sense of relief.

6

Andy believed that Geoff and Ralph had missed something. Either that, or they had a bias that made them misread the facts. The doctors giving this party didn't erect deliberate barriers against male nurses who chatted-up the girls. So far as Andy could tell – and he had checked it carefully during the half hour he had been there – the male nurses' behaviour was curtailed only when they got unruly. It had nothing to do with keeping them away from the ladies. It just so happened that, when a male nurse did misbehave, the breach was usually in connection with some female or other.

It wasn't a bad bit of observation, Andy thought, considering he had sunk probably half a bottle of wine in thirty-five minutes.

'I'm not drunk, mind you,' he pointed out to June Reilly, who had wandered across to him a minute earlier. She had jokingly remarked that he was putting away the plonk at a rate of knots. 'It's simple physics,' Andy went on. 'A man my size can hold it – my liver's bigger so the drink gets processed faster. The rate of diffusion's higher, too, because there's more of me to spread it around in . . .'

June was nodding, intrigued by the fact that, because Andy *was* rather drunk, he was measurably transformed. So far, she had only ever seen him unbend properly in the presence of children. In his present state of inebriation, Andy displayed a lot of unexpected charm. His manner was cool, he actually looked her straight in the eye and he didn't speak nearly so fast as usual. There was also a fleeting, lopsided little smile that June found attractive.

'It's really hopping in here, isn't it?' Andy said.

'The harder you work, the harder you play,' June observed. 'That's the case with medics, anyway.'

They were in a long, deep-carpeted room in one of the best houses in Walford. It belonged to a solicitor who was related to Dr Gupta, whose leaving party this was. The furniture was almost forbiddingly luxurious – ornate side tables, brocaded chairs and couches, heavy, richly-shaded lamps.

'This is one of the better parties, mind you,' June said. 'The organizers have taken a lot of trouble to make it work, for a change.'

The air was filled with music. It was loud but it was also superbly reproduced, so it didn't grate on the ears. Nobody had to shout to make themselves heard. Upwards of forty drinking, laughing, chattering people were either gathered in wide-spaced groups, or huddling here and there in pairs, or dancing in twos, threes and fours. Others were simply drifting from point to point.

At present Andy was leaning against the wall by the ornate fireplace, nursing his glass. June Reilly, transformed wondrously by upswept hair, smooth cosmetics and a ravishingly tight black pilot suit, was standing directly in front of him. She had a hand on her hip and her feet were spread, as if this was a showdown. She, too, had consumed quite a lot of wine.

'I'm surprised there's so many male nurses here,' Andy remarked. His mind was still partly on the private observation he had made.

'Surprised? Why?'

He shrugged. 'I'd sort of been led to believe they weren't all that welcome at these functions.'

'That's balls,' June said without emphasis. 'How many men are on the nursing strength at the King George? Thirty, maybe? You can usually guarantee more than half of them'll show up at the parties – invited or not.'

Andy didn't feel like mentioning his observation about their behaviour, but he discovered he was doing it anyway. 'They're boisterous, a lot of them. I mean plenty of people here are boisterous, but – '

'But the male nurses are more inclined to act the goat and get rowdy.'

Andy nodded. 'Little Doc Malik's ticked off a couple of them already.'

'More than a couple of them'll get chucked out before the night's over.' June looked around her for a moment. 'A lot of men definitely get social hang-ups about being in nursing.'

'You can hardly blame them,' Andy murmured, 'what with some of the wisecracks you have to put up with from other men, and quite a few women – '

'I know, I know. It can be tough, but some blokes learn to take it in their stride, don't they? The others start feeling like second-class citizens. They behave the same way downtrodden kids do when they come up against a social threat.'

Andy sipped his drink. 'Sometimes it's hard to avoid feeling . . .' He thought for a moment. 'Insecure. Or as you said, second class. I mean, think about it.' He made a wide, vague gesture with his glass, as if he was about to conduct a fanfare. 'You work like a pack horse for laughable wages. You study as hard as you labour. You give the job every ounce of your patience and understanding. What happens? You wind up with about as much status as as the man who cleans out the toilets.'

June frowned. 'That's a teensy bit of an exaggeration – '

'Is it? I'm at the beck and call of any patient who needs a bedpan, right? But worse than that, a lot worse, is that any clown of a houseman has the right to turn round and shove me about, or just put me down if he feels like it.'

'That happens to female nurses too, remember. It's not a special hardship reserved for the men.'

'They get more of a kick out of doing it to the men,' Andy said stubbornly.

'Look.' June pointed to the corner by the big bay window. Two final-year male nurses were forcing their clumsy, intoxicated attentions on a pair of young nurses who clearly didn't want anything to do with them. 'You're not trying to condone that kind of nonsense, are you?'

'No, I'm not,' Andy said. 'What I'm doing is brushing up on my compassion. Just like Dr Norris said I should.'

'There are limits to compassion.' June reached and took his glass, which Andy was surprised to see was empty. 'I'll get you a refill.'

He watched her weave between two groups of people and skirt past some dancers. June had a very confident swing to her hips, he thought. It was provocative. It was also challenging, just like that look she sometimes had. He remembered what Ralph had said about her; she was strictly a doctor's dolly. He wondered now if that was sour grapes, or simply a wrong assessment, like his flatmates' views on doctors' parties.

A minute later he saw the steady-eyed challenge again as June came back with his fresh drink. What did she expect of him, he wondered. Was he supposed to make a pass at her? He wasn't sure he even knew what a pass was.

'Have you done any circulating yet?' she asked him, handing over the glass.

'I've said hello to a couple of people.'

'Get some more of that down you and I'll introduce you to Wanda.'

'Wanda?'

'A friend of mine.'

He suddenly remembered what June had said the first day he met her; 'We'll soon fix you up.' Was this it? Was it going to happen right now? *Right now*? Andy took a deep gulp from his glass.

'Over here,' June said, leading him towards a couch that had been obscured by a clutch of chattering girls. Andy walked cautiously behind June, feeling his heart-rate take a panicky climb as he saw the girl sitting there. She was tall, fine-featured and terribly haughty looking. Desperately confident too. She wasn't for beginners, Andy thought. She'd reduce him to a bumbling jelly inside minutes. He took another slurp of wine.

'Here we are,' June said brightly. 'Wanda Brandys, this is Andy O'Brien.'

There was a moment of intense confusion, a moment in which Andy was sure he stood gawping like an idiot. June wasn't introducing him to the haughty one on the couch. She was holding out her arm towards a small, timid-looking creature standing at the far end of the couch. The girl simultaneously smiled and frowned as Andy blinked at her.

'Sorry . . .' He extended his hand, feeling a rush of relief. The girl's small fingers closed lightly on his. 'Nice to meet you, Wanda.'

'Wanda's my neighbour – across the hall. She's a social

55

worker.' June switched her smile back and forth between them for a moment, then shot a glance across the room. She nodded to somebody beyond the smokescreen. 'I'll catch up with you later,' she said, just as brightly as before. She was gone before Andy realized it.

'Well, now . . .' He raised his glass but only let the wine splash his lip this time. It was a way of playing for time. Wanda whatsername didn't look at all menacing. She had a hesitant manner that went well with her quiet prettiness. The hairstyle was modern but distinctly low-key. Her dress was plain and had a high neck. A modest girl, Andy decided.

'June tells me you have just come to London from Scotland.'

'That's right.' He tried to place the accent. German, maybe. 'How long have you been here?'

'Oh, eleven years now. Since I was thirteen.'

Nothing really shy about her, Andy thought as he nodded interestedly at the information. Firm delivery, steady gaze. But no threat, no hint of challenge. 'Where did you come from?'

'Poland. My whole family came away when things began to get – difficult.'

He hoped she didn't want to talk about politics. 'What branch of social work are you in?'

'I deal with children – just as you do.'

'Oh, really.' He felt himself relaxing.

The process of relaxation underwent a slow change over the following two hours. With a further three or four glasses of wine in him, Andy realized he had simply become a part of the general tempo. He had stopped checking on himself to see how he felt, or how he stood in relation to the others.

Lots of things had contributed to his numb, pleasant

euphoria. Wine had, certainly. The surrounding distractions, too. There had been the fiasco of Dr Gupta, tubby, benign and seriously drunk, trying to copy some Charleston steps from two other revellers. He ended up on his back, bewildered, beside the remains of a coffee table that his elbow dismantled on his way down. There had been the eventual noisy eviction of the two male nurses who had been bothering the girls. And everyone had roared with laughter as the owner of the house tripped during a vigorous dance routine and galloped smartly, sideways, into the wall.

Most of all, though, it had been the presence of little Wanda that had soothed Andy into his state of contented wellbeing. She had stuck with him, showing no interest in anyone else. He had found that talking to her was easy, and the talk was absorbing without taxing him in any way. She was enthusiastic about her work, and she had very positive views about society and life in general.

'Too many people trap themselves in the fight for security,' she said at one point. 'Just like Shaw said, man is a dying animal, yes? He can't have much security anyway, not in the end. So why should he make himself miserable trying to find a safety that doesn't exist?'

Andy had liked that. He wasn't sure if he agreed with it, but it had a nice, well considered, rounded sound to it. So had something else she said; 'People in the West are like sailing boats. The flow of cash is the wind. If you can understand the wind, it makes their movements easy to predict.'

On the subject of children, though, Wanda was superb. She had made a lot of profound observations about them. 'They're the most oppressed people in any society,' she said. Later, when Andy had talked about how sick kids had much more courage than many a less-sick adult, she

57

nodded and said, 'We have a grasp of life when we're young. But we're in no position then to control things. Our talent gets corrupted by the time we grow up. We simply get on with the business of corrupting the next generation.'

Heady stuff, Andy thought. And all so calmly stated, without aggression or bitterness or – highly important – any sign of wanting to argue with him. She had a good fund of social grace. Andy liked Wanda a lot.

People began leaving towards midnight. Watching the drift, Andy decided he'd better take his leave, too. He wondered if he should suggest seeing Wanda again. After wondering about it for another minute, he decided he shouldn't. When he was sober he would probably be terrified at the thought of taking her out.

'I brought June in my car,' Wanda said, looking around. 'I don't see her anywhere. It looks as if someone else has given her a lift back.' She turned to Andy. 'Perhaps I could offer you a lift?'

'Well. I'm living on Carver Road – that might be a bit out of your way.'

'Not at all.'

Five minutes later Andy was sitting beside Wanda in her little Fiat, watching her confidently steer her way through Walford's dimly lit streets.

'It has been pleasant meeting you, Andy,' she said.

'I've enjoyed myself too, Wanda.'

'We get on well together.' Not a trace of awkwardness, he observed, nor coyness. A plain fact, plainly stated. 'Perhaps we should see each other again.' After a pause she glanced at him. 'If you would want that, of course.'

He was sure he did, although he still felt he could trust his instincts a lot better in sober daylight. Why did it have to be such a territory of fear for him, this business of going out with girls? He had asked himself the question so often he didn't even try to come up with an answer now.

'You've become very quiet,' Wanda murmured.

'Sorry.' He pulled himself together and tried to imagine seeing her again. On reflection, she certainly was one of the few girls he had ever been able to relax with. No challenge. No waiting for him to make some vital move. She made him feel safe. 'When would you like to go out again, then?'

The car stopped. 'Coffee?' She pointed at the steps outside. 'I live here.'

A bubble of panic bounced across Andy's stomach. 'Well . . .' He pretended to look at his watch.

'Forgive me,' Wanda said easily. 'It was just a suggestion. I thought you might have liked some of my expresso.'

'Of course I would,' he heard himself say.

They went up a dark staircase and stopped outside facing doors on the second landing. There was music and giggling from behind the door on the left.

'June,' Wanda said.

Andy listened and heard a man's laugh. He was sure he recognized it. Maybe she was a doctor's dolly after all.

The interior of Wanda's flat was bright and sparely furnished. 'Sit down,' she told Andy. 'I'll go and put on the machine.'

He sat on the orange-and-grey couch and stared at the three framed photographs on the opposite wall. They were family portraits, he guessed; a grey-haired man with an expression as formal as his suit, a slightly younger-looking woman with traces of Wanda in her features, and a picture of both the man and woman with the young, maybe ten-year-old Wanda between them.

'Only a few minutes to wait,' Wanda said, coming back from the kitchen. She stood for a moment looking at Andy. In this light she looked much less timid than she had at the party. He guessed it was because she was used to simple surroundings. Opulence probably made her uncomfortable. 'This is nice,' she said, smiling a little. 'I like it when people can get on easily and don't have to skulk behind façades.'

Andy nodded. 'Very nice.' He had managed not to blush.

She went off again, along the small passage that linked with the hallway. Andy sat back with his hands behind his head, studying the books now, neatly racked on two long shelves. There was nothing he recognized, apart from *Palgrave's Golden Treasury*. Suddenly he was thinking about himself again. Here he was, sitting in a girl's flat while she made him coffee. There had been no dread build-up, no difficulty. He should have known that this kind of thing was possible. It wasn't all terrible games and ominous preludes.

When Wanda returned she breezed straight through to the kitchen. She was in her dressing gown, Andy noticed. A very modest dressing gown, though – heavy and woolly and so long it trailed on the floor. He heard a click, then she came back. To his slight discomfort she stood directly in front of him, as June had done earlier.

'Andy.' She had said his name, no more. It was the firmness in her eyes that was unnerving. 'I'm sure we agree – we seem to do on a lot of other things – that falseness is bad for any relationship.'

She'd said that already, hadn't she, when she talked about skulking behind façades? But now she'd said relationship. Those eyes were very open now, terribly

60

candid. Andy's mind raced, trying to figure out what was happening here. *Relationship*?

'It's silly to play into the hands of convention, with all its stupid formalities,' She glanced towards the kitchen. 'I've put the coffee machine on hold.'

As her eyes returned to him Andy realized, with a terrible jolt, that the dressing gown was untied. In the shadowy opening her naked body gloamed its terrifying challenge. He gulped. This was all wrong. It was like an ambush. Coffee she'd said, a cup of coffee, and suddenly he was being expected to go to bed with her. That *was* what she expected, wasn't it?

'Wanda . . . I . . .' Suffering God, he *had* been fixed up! June had put him on to a Polish raver! Andy felt himself stand up, shifting out of the line of that gap in her dressing gown. 'Don't misunderstand me,' he croaked.

'What's wrong?' Her eyes looked genuinely troubled.

'It's just that I don't . . .'

'What?'

He shook his head as if there was something lodged in his hair. 'Look, I don't want to offend you.' He watched her eyes narrow. 'This – us. I mean, I need time to – '

'To bow to convention?' Her Polish gutturals had suddenly hardened. 'To observe bourgeois niceties?' With a swift movement she did up the belt of her robe. 'Obviously I misunderstood.' She gazed at the vacant couch.

'It's not that I'm that worried about convention, Wanda . . .'

Her silence was terrible. He felt as bad now as he had ever felt with any woman. Worse. He hadn't seen the challenge coming so he hadn't sidestepped in time. He had been confronted by it and had failed – miserably, as he probably always would.

'Sorry,' he said.

'Don't be,' she replied coldly. She tightened the belt another inch and looked at him. 'The error was mine, Andy. Wine damages my judgement, I should bear that in mind.' Without another word, she turned and walked off along the passage. He heard a door close.

On the street he looked about him, confused. Left, he decided after a minute and began walking.

His mind felt like a great big throbbing sore. Every thought either jarred or stung. This thing, this awful separateness from what everybody else was up to all the time – it was going to damage him seriously, he was sure of that. So far it had only made life occasionally difficult. Now, immersed in a society where it was less easy than before to keep his life private, his deficiency was bound to come under scrutiny. Word would get round – Andy O'Brien, twenty-five, professionally qualified, fit and healthy except for a chronic, probably incurable case of virginity.

As the misery deepened he walked more slowly, hearing his feet echo on the empty streets. After ten minutes he stopped, looked around him and heaved a long, groaning sigh. It was bad enough that the evening had put a scar on his personality. Bad enough that he felt like something weird, unsavoury and incomplete. Was that truly not enough, he thought, without the aggravation of finding himself on a strange street in a strange part of Walford, completely lost?

7

The date stamp came down on the blotter with a smart thump. Over her shoulder Debbie heard Cynthia, the head cashier say, 'Is that your way of making time go backwards?'

Debbie looked at the blue-printed date. 'What's wrong with it? Today's the twelfth, isn't it?'

'Of May.'

Debbie looked again. It said April. 'Oh, pooh.' She opened the baseplate and made the adjustment to the little rubber belt. 'The month must have changed when I altered the date.'

'Uhuh.' Cynthia put on her grumpy-auntie look. 'Your mind's elsewhere this morning. That's your second cock-up and we're not even open yet.'

Debbie wished Cynthia wouldn't say cock-up. It sounded obscene. She was always saying balls-up, too. She'd even been heard to refer to one of the customers as a dick-head. 'I'm sorry, Cynth. My attention *is* a bit divided, as it happens.'

'Worried about your interview with Dowson?'

Debbie nodded. The previous afternoon the manager had told her he wanted to see her in his room at eleven-thirty this morning. 'I can't imagine what it's about.'

'You'll know soon enough.' Cynthia wandered away to the other end of the counter.

The trouble with Mr Dowson, in Debbie's experience, was that he never gave clues. He could usher you into the office with his customarily calm, almost preoccupied face and then blow up at you; with the same look he could call you in and hand out the warmest congratulations. Right now, Debbie had a niggling worry that he wanted to talk to her about her examination performance.

That was another mystery in itself. The last paper she had sat was very odd. She had found herself answering all the questions, practically without hesitating. She even finished before time. Cynthia had said she was just getting better at understanding the course, but Debbie wasn't buying that. Anything so easy had to be worrying, there had to be something wildly wrong somewhere. She chewed her lip absently as she began setting up her till.

'All right then are we, Debbles?'

It was George, the new junior, a youth with a lardy complexion, bad breath and the undying conviction that most of the girls in the bank fancied him, in spite of all the contrary evidence.

'You can call me Miss Wilkins, Deborah, or Debbie. But *not* Debbles. All right?'

'Oh.' George's eyebrows shot up. 'One of them days, is it?' He tried to melt her frown with his warmest smile, which was marred by a purple crack on his bottom lip. 'Whose bed did you get out on the wrong side of this mornin', eh?'

'Don't be so rude.' Debbie banged down a plastic bag of fifty pences and snatched up a wad of pound notes.

George moved closer. 'What d'you call a Welshman with a stick up his bum?'

'George!'

'No. Taffy Apple.' He let out a noise midway between a snuffle and a giggle.

Blushing, Debbie stomped away to the stationery cupboard. There were times, she would admit, when George could amuse her. This wasn't one of those times. This was an occasion when he was such a slimy irritant she could easily enough slap him.

'Hoi, you. Grot Bag,' Cynthia called out, using one of her many names for George. 'Get on with your own work and leave other people to do theirs.'

Debbie reflected that there were some gratifying aspects to Cynthia's coarseness. She watched George move off and went back to her till. No more than a couple of minutes passed before she was interrupted again. It was Trudie this time.

'Sorry to bother you . . .' The junior held up a clipped sheaf of papers. 'It's about the sports.'

'What about them?'

'I'm to get a list of the events you're takin' part in.'

Debbie wished she had never agreed to take part. The only reason she had, of course, was because it looked good on a bank employee's record if he or she displayed plenty of team spirit.

'You're down for the hundred metres,' Trudie murmured, frowning at the top sheet of paper. 'Miss Hickson over at personnel 'phoned to ask if that's a mistake.'

Debbie glared at the girl. 'What does she mean by that? Of course it isn't a mistake. I'm pretty good in the hundred metres.'

Trudie shook her head and tapped the papers. 'No. She means is it a mistake that you're only down for the one event.'

'No, it's not,' Debbie snapped.

'Because everybody else from this branch, them that's takin' part I mean, they're all doin' a minimum three events.'

Debbie felt her mood darken. 'Three? I was told I could please myself what I did.'

Trudie nodded. ''Course you can. Miss Hickson just

thinks it'll look odd that you're the only one from here that's not – '

'Oh all right.' Miss Hickson was an interfering, warty old bag, Debbie thought fiercely. 'What other events does she suggest I go in for? The pole vault? Tossing the caber?'

Trudie looked hurt. 'I just take the phone messages, Debbie. It's not my fault what she says . . .'

'I know.' Debbie forced a smile that spread no further than her mouth. 'Sorry, Trudie. Let's have a look at the sheets.'

It was crazy to think that her future in banking could be damaged, however subtly, if she showed less enthusiasm for sports than some of her colleagues. But that was the way it went. No sense in bucking the system. She ran her eye along the list of events, twice, then said, 'Put me down for the long jump and, um, the relay.' Might as well go the whole hog and burn herself out for her masters, she thought, handing back the sheets.

'Right you are.' Trudie made the appropriate marks. 'Thanks.' Rather hesitantly, she added, 'I've to remind you about the meetin' on Friday night – '

'Meeting? God, Trudie, is there any end to all this?'

'It's a meetin' at Regional Head Office to get the plans for the sports day sorted out. There's a memo on the bulletin board.'

Debbie sighed. 'OK, fine, I'll be there.'

The bank doors were being unlocked as Trudie moved away. Debbie's till still wasn't ready. She groaned softly as she threw notes and coins into the recesses. It was easy to see the pattern this day would take. It would be one irritation and vexation after another. The die was cast. And at the back of it all there was the baleful black cloud, her appointment with the manager. Debbie glanced up from her till, trying to look cheerful and competent as the first surly-looking customers shuffled in.

Three-and-a-half hours later Mr Young, the proprietor of a small vegetarian restaurant called *True Grits* was asked by a smiling, attractive, once-a-week luncheon customer if he would recommend something for a sudden and ravening appetite.

'Well now.' Young set his elbow on the edge of the counter and scratched his hairless scalp. 'What you want, I'd say, takin' the weather into account of course, is the six-juice cocktail, followed by the bean salad, then a nice cracked wheat risotto – with a dollop of puréed potato if you're really starvin'.'

'Sold,' Debbie said.

Mr Young pointed to a sunlit table by the window. 'Go an' sit yourself down, love. I'll bring it across in a jiffy.'

It was wonderful, Debbie thought as she made her way through the cluster of other tables, how one bright event could transform a day. Immediately after the chat with the manager, she had noticed the difference. She served one pleasant customer after another. She had to do nothing for them that was complicated, annoying or time-consuming. Time, nevertheless, was consumed at amazing speed. It was lunchtime before she knew it and she had acquired a robust hunger, right out of the blue.

She recognized a customer at a nearby table, a skinny, blotchy-faced woman. Debbie smiled at her and the customer smiled back. Being a bank clerk felt like fun again. It felt satisfying, fulfilling. All because of a five-minute meeting with the manager.

'I can't tell you anything specific, Debbie,' Mr Dowson had said, 'because nothing specific was said to me. I can only tell you that as I was getting ready to leave yesterday,

I had a call from a Local Director to say that the overall standard of your written examination work is looking splendid. Furthermore, he told me that the forthcoming branch-inspectors' report will also mention you favourably.' At that point the manager bestowed one of his rare smiles. 'The Director thought I would like to know, and I thought you would, too.'

The afterglow felt strong enough to last her for the rest of the week. *They're pleased with me*! she thought gleefully. She imagined a boardroom full of Directors, beaming and nodding admiringly as they passed her exam papers round the table. *I'm getting on*! The knowledge of it made her feel capable of anything. In a mood like this, Debbie reckoned she could be persuaded to listen to half a dozen of George's mucky jokes without even wincing – and put her name down for another couple of sports day events while she was at it.

By the time she was on to the risotto the sense of gratified hunger was nicely balancing her feeling of self satisfaction. She mustn't overdo that, she reminded herself; to be self-content was to be static. She should watch out for the satisfied appetite bit, too. The waistline would start shifting and that would never do. She smiled apologetically across the restaurant to Mr Young as she slid the half-eaten plateful away from her. She thought for a moment, then signalled that she would like some of the establishment's acclaimed de-caffeinated coffee.

The customer who had recognized her got up to leave. As she passed Debbie's table she stopped.

'I didn't know you were vegetarian, Miss Wilkins.'

'I'm not. But I've managed to kid myself it's good for me once a week.'

A thin skein of disapproval crossed the woman's eyes. 'It's not something to be treated lightly,' she said. 'I don't know how I'd be if I hadn't stopped eating meat and dairy products.'

A lot healthier-looking, Debbie thought. 'I don't have your will-power,' she chirped. 'A hamburger's still pretty irresistible to me, I'm afraid.'

The woman smiled but managed to retain the disapproving look. 'Perhaps one day you'll take your diet more seriously, my dear.'

'I'll let you know when I do,' Debbie said sweetly, watching her go.

Like most encounters with bank customers, the exchange had done little to alter Debbie's mood. She sat with her coffee cup between both hands and stared contentedly out at the street, slowly relishing the day's developments. She didn't hear the door open and close again. She didn't hear the polite exchange at the counter, nor did she see the man approach with his coffee and sit down adjacent to her, his back to the rest of the room.

'Well then, Debbie.'

She almost dropped her cup. Colin Borrowfield was smiling at her, craning his head in a sleek gesture of greeting. Debbie glanced anxiously at the counter. Mr Young was busy with another customer.

'I've been away for a few weeks,' Borrowfield said. 'Hamburg, actually. Business.'

Debbie hadn't known that. She had assumed he'd given up pestering her. It had been so long she'd almost managed to forget how much he had scared her.

'Has that coffee paralysed your tongue?' he asked, making his faultless grin. 'It doesn't surprise me. Terrible stuff.'

Alongside her nervousness, Debbie felt that wonderment again; how could a man who looked like that be such a slug?

'I caught sight of you as I was parking the car,' Borrowfield said, pointing to the red Porsche across the road. 'Couldn't go past without saying hello.'

'Well you've said it now,' Debbie husked bravely.

Borrowfield sighed and sipped his coffee. 'This is no way to go on, is it?' He reached out and put a hand on her arm, startling her. 'I'm determined we'll get along.'

'Please leave me alone.' Trembling, Debbie put down the cup, making it rattle on the saucer. 'Please. I've told you before – '

'And I've told you. You're getting me all wrong.'

His eyes said differently. Debbie stared at them. She felt fouled by his gaze. 'Why . . .'

'Yes?'

'Why do you keep it up?'

The nastiness spread momentarily to his entire face. It was a leer of deliberate misunderstanding. 'Bit of a personal question isn't it, Debbie?'

She gritted her teeth and looked around. It was as if there was a conspiracy among the other diners. Not one of them was looking her way. It made her feel trapped. 'How can you keep pestering somebody who doesn't want to know?' Her voice was as shaky as her hands.

'It's the evangelist in me. I know you'll see the light, if I'm persistent enough.'

With an effort Debbie pushed back her chair and lifted her handbag. As she stood up Borrowfield switched his grip to her wrist. This time the grasp was firmer, detaining her.

'I'll see you around,' he murmured. He wasn't smiling now. He was showing her a look she had seen once before, years ago, when she was a little girl. A man had stood before her fleetingly as she waited for her mother outside a shop. He had swept his coat aside briefly . . .

'Please let me go,' Debbie hissed, driving away the hideous memory.

'Oh come on, now . . .'

'If you bother me again,' she wavered, 'I'm going to report you.' Tears stung her eyes as the immaculate fingers withdrew.

'And who would believe you?' His eyes bored into hers. 'I've a very strong reputation around here, Debbie. I'm well respected. Who'd even start to believe anything unpleasant a little slip of a bank girl might say about me?' His voice lowered. 'I know your manager certainly wouldn't.'

Debbie made to move off.

'Think what it could do to your future over there,' Borrowfield went on. 'Especially if I was to explain – reluctantly, of course – that you'd been paying me a bit too much attention lately.' He shook his head. 'Some girls get funny ideas, don't they? Especially when a personable, well-off man rebuffs them.' As he stood up he switched on his smile again and said, 'How are you enjoying it in that big flat of yours, by the way?'

Debbie swept away towards the counter, fumbling open her purse. *He knows where I live*! The awful fact numbed her as she tried to understand what Mr Young was saying.

'Two ninety-eight with the coffee, love.'

She gulped, looked into her purse and looked back at him. 'Sorry?'

He repeated himself. It registered. Debbie gave him three pound notes. Borrowfield appeared beside her and put down the money for his coffee. He nodded amiably at Mr Young and leaned close to Debbie.

'Be seeing you,' he murmured as he moved off.

It was only a small relief to hear the door close. Debbie

71

made a fuss of closing her bag, giving him time to clear off.

'Nice gentleman, that,' Young said. Debbie stared at him. 'Your friend, love. Pleasant type. He comes in here quite a bit.'

'Does he?' Debbie found herself heading for the door, clutching her handbag to her like a shield. I won't be coming back then, she thought.

On the street she saw the Porsche pull away. Borrowfield was waving. Debbie pretended not to see. As she waited by the crossing she felt a strong impulse to cry. He was back. Borrowfield was there again, hovering, menacing. He had ruined her day. Worse, he had taken away her confidence and put back fear in its place.

8

During the third week in May, one month after Andy had gone to work in London, he wrote to his foster parents for the second time. Jenny sat at the kitchen table and listened intently as her husband, Tom, read out the letter.

'I believe, at long last, that I'm properly settled,' Andy wrote. 'The work is interesting, in fact it's often fascinating. My flatmates, Geoff Mercer and Ralph Dixon, are both good sorts and they've introduced me to a pretty active social life here, which I pursue as often as I'm able. Frankly, at the end of most shifts all I'm ready for is my bed.'

'Just like when he was here,' Jenny murmured. 'He was always one to work hard. Never a shirker.'

Tom nodded and read on. 'Twice a week I play squash at a local club. When I have a free Saturday night I go to the wine bar and, occasionally, to an Italian bistro with Geoff and one or two of the crowd. They're a lot different from the people and places I used to know in Glasgow – no better or worse, just different. The people in Walford are friendly in the main and my working relationships are all pretty good.'

Tom looked at Jenny over the rims of his reading glasses. 'Sounds like he's fitting in, eh?'

Jenny nodded. Her expression suggested she was a little disappointed at that.

Clearing his throat, Tom started on the remainder of the letter. 'We've got some very sad cases here. One, a child born to an alcoholic mother, died yesterday after surviving nearly five weeks. I've never seen anything quite so terrible as that baby's suffering. I can't say, either, that I've come across any creature so callously indifferent as the mother. A Consultant here says I should have compassion for people like her. I have to confess, after seeing the offhand way she took the news of the child's death, that my sharpest impulse was to shake her until her teeth rattled. For her poor, broken husband, on the other hand, I had nothing but compassion. Helpless compassion, I have to add. His position seems as hopeless and negative as his wife's.

'But on to brighter things. I'm taking part in a sports meeting this Saturday. It's between staff from East London hospitals and people from various branches of a big bank. I'll be in the five-a-side football (naturally!) and the long jump. Keep your fingers crossed for me.'

Andy closed with a few words about missing them and expressed the hope that he would be able to see them before too long, though he specified no probable dates.

'It's always nice to get word,' Tom said quietly as he folded the letter and put it down. He eyed Jenny cautiously. She was frowning at the tablecloth. 'What's the matter?'

'Nothing. It just makes me start wearying for him a bit more, getting a letter.'

'He's a grown man, Jenny. He's out in the world, conducting his own life, following his own career. It's what we worked for, isn't it? We raised him to this. You should be pleased.'

'Oh, I'm pleased for the boy all right. Pleased he's happy and getting on.' She looked up. 'He sounds like he's definitely going to settle in London, doesn't he?'

Tom nodded. His look was only fractionally less sad

than Jenny's, in spite of the positive, encouraging tone he had tried to impart. 'It's maybe early to say that, but yes, it sounds as if he's found his slot – for a while, anyway.'

After a moment Jenny said, 'Maybe we could go down and see him some time. Just for a day or two.'

'Now Jenny . . .'

'I don't mean we should interfere. I meant we could go there if he was too busy to come up.'

Tom hesitated for a minute, then decided he should say what he was thinking. 'You're going to have to let him go. It's the only way you'll hang on to his affection. And his respect.' It was not an easy thing for Tom to say. It made him flush slightly. He noticed, though, that Jenny was nodding.

'I know what you mean.' She sighed. 'I'm possessive. I know that.'

She rose, intending to cover her rush of feelings by going to the cooker and stirring the dinner. She didn't make it. Turning to pass Tom she let out a sob too big to hold. She threw her arms about him.

'There, there.' He patted her shoulder, looking down at her head pressed tight against his pullover. 'It'll get better,' he said softly. 'Time, Jenny. It mends every hurt.'

'I know that too,' she said, catching her breath. 'I'll be honest with you, though.' She moved back, mopping her eyes with the back of her hand. 'No matter what you say, and sore as it is, I don't want to stop missing my big daft boy.'

Tom nodded, understanding perfectly. He condoned her unreasonable, self-wounding attitude. It was practically identical to his own. There were moments in life, after all, when cold logic didn't deserve a look in.

* * *

Young, aggressive, overweight Amanda had been shouting when it happened. Now she sat on a chair in the playroom, mouth gaping, eyes wide and frightened, while a dozen other children gathered round to stare at her. Staff Nurse Reilly pushed her way through the little throng and looked at Amanda.

'What happened?'

'She was just bawlin',' a little boy offered.

'Bawling?'

'At Winston.'

June Reilly turned her attention to a gangly West Indian lad with a leg brace. 'Why was she bawling at you? Did you do anything after she bawled?'

Winston shook his head fearfully. 'Ah dint do nothin'. She wus callin' me a gimpy spade 'cause Ah won at Cluedo.'

'A *cheatin'* gimpy spade,' another boy corrected. 'She reckoned Winston took a peek at the cards.'

'Ah nevvuh did.'

'I know,' the boy said dispassionately. They all returned their attention to Amanda, who was still wide-mouthed, silent and scared looking.

June touched the child's face. 'Amanda, can you move your chin at all? Can you waggle it from side to side?'

Amanda tried. The jaw didn't budge, but she croaked and big tears appeared at the corners of her eyes.

'God,' June sighed. 'As if I wasn't busy enough. Look Amanda, just sit tight and we'll get you wheeled over to Casualty. You're going to be all right, OK? Just don't move. The rest of you, get out of my feet.'

As she turned to leave Andy came into the playroom.

'You look harassed,' he said pleasantly.

'It's Amanda. She's dislocated her jaw. I'm going for a

76

wheelchair – it's not safe to hump anything that size all the way across to Cas.'

'Let's have a look.'

Andy went to where the child sat stiffly in her chair, rolling her eyes from side to side, trying to see what was going on. Andy patted her shoulder, told her not to worry, then squatted in front of her. He felt either side of her jaw then beckoned June to come across.

'Stand beside her, will you? Just to reassure her.'

'Are you going to try it on your own?'

'Don't see why not.'

June shrugged and took up her position to the side of Amanda.

'Right now,' Andy grunted. 'Hold tight, darling, and we'll soon have you out of this fix.'

He took a gauze pack from his breast pocket, tore it open and made a pad for each thumb. He placed the padded thumbs on Amanda's lower back teeth and pressed down hard. His fingers went under her chin and eased their way gently up into the angle of her jaw. There was a little click and Amanda yelped. When Andy took away his thumbs she was able to close her mouth.

'There now. All better.'

Amanda blinked at him resentfully. 'That was bleedin' sore.' She rubbed her jaw with both hands.

'Serves you right for calling Winston names,' June chided her.

'Well . . .' Amanda sniffed noisily and knuckled her eyes. 'The rotten git *was* cheatin'. He had to be . . .'

'That's enough talk for now, Andy told her. 'You'll have to keep your mouth shut for a while. Till tea time, anyway.' He saw the protest rise in Amanda's throat. 'If you don't, we'll have to bandage it shut.'

When they were sure order had been restored to the

playroom, Andy and June went back to the ward. 'I'll be glad when that Amanda's diabetes gets balanced and we can send her home,' June said as they stood for a moment and watched the other nurses going about their duties.

'She's quite the holy terror,' Andy murmured.

'And bully and bigot and all-round monster,' June added. 'And she's only eleven. If it wasn't for my undermining streak of sympathy for the little beast, I'd have enjoyed seeing her stuck like that for a while longer.' She glanced thoughtfully at Andy. 'I suppose you know, by the way, that you're not supposed to reduce a dislocated jaw.'

He nodded easily. 'I know. Strictly the doctor's province. But I've done it plenty of times. Drunks are always getting their big mouths jammed open – it's every man to the pumps on a busy Saturday night at the Glasgow Royal.'

June consulted her watch. 'Fancy a cuppa? Beattie's nipped off for half an hour.' She winked. 'A bit of the old illicit, if you ask me.'

Andy went with her to the sluice and helped get a pot of coffee ready. While they waited for the water to heat June eased herself on to the work top and fished out her cigarettes.

'Aren't you curious?' she asked Andy through a cloud of smoke. She shook the match out and watched him closely, one eye narrowed against the fumes.

'What about?'

'Sister. Her little weakness.'

'You said you'd wise me up when you got to know me better.'

June inhaled deeply, held on to the smoke for a moment, then expelled it at speed towards the floor. 'Tell you what,' she said, in a scheming tone that made Andy instantly wary, 'you satisfy my curiosity and I'll satisfy yours.'

Andy tried to look nonchalantly detached from any need to know anything.

'What do you say?' June prompted.

He had a powerful suspicion about where her interest lay. 'It depends what you want to know.'

'You and Wanda. How did it go?'

He had thought that was it. Since the excruciating embarrassment of that night, Andy had waited for June to say something. Until now she hadn't, although he'd had the feeling from time to time that she was about to raise the matter. Now that she had, he did what he had planned to do all along; he tried to look puzzled.

'You're not telling me you've forgotten, have you?'

'That party . . .' He waved his hand. 'A lot of what happened is just a jumble.'

'Wanda's said nothing. That's not like her.'

So, he mused, if anything had happened, it would have been broadcast. Nice to know.

'Well?'

'I told you, it's all a jumble . . .'

'Aw, that's bullshit, Andy. I was only wondering if you made it with her, that's all.' She grinned. 'Old Wanda's a bit of a man eater on the quiet.'

Busying himself with the coffee, he said, 'Is that why you introduced me to her?'

June nodded. 'It was kindly meant.'

He poured two cups and passed June's to her. 'All right,' he said. 'I'll square with you. Nothing happened.' This was the second part of what he had planned to do all along, courage permitting.

'Truly?'

He nodded.

'Why not? Scare you a bit, did she?'

Andy observed the impish glimmer in her eye. 'No. She didn't scare me at all. But I like to work for my supper, if you get my drift.' Still watching her, he decided tentatively that it had worked. If there was anything showing on her face, it was a shred of respect.

'Oh, I see,' June stared at her cup for a moment. 'Look, I'm sorry if I put you in the kind of situation you don't like. I was only trying to be – '

'Kind?'

'No, I wouldn't put it like that, exactly . . .'

Andy smiled. 'I'll take it as neighbourly, then. But believe me June, I can attend to my own requirements in that direction. OK?'

She looked chastened. 'Sure.' She drank her coffee, not meeting his eyes any more. After a decent silence, she said, 'About our Beattie . . .'

'It's the Hospital Secretary's assistant, isn't it? Little Miss Pomphrey with the bad leg.'

She blinked. 'How the hell did you find out?'

'Same way as you. Keen observation, backed by experience, confirmed by careful deduction. I've been in this game as long as you, remember. Competent nurses are usually red-hot detectives.'

Later, as he set up a tray of instruments for a lumbar puncture, Andy had time to reflect on that little exchange with June. She had gone away with no wind left in her sails. He had managed to con her splendidly, he thought.

'The truth can be presented in as many ways as a lie, and often to more devastating effect.' That was what Andy's favourite tutor had told his psychology class. 'There are even those who have been convinced, beyond the wisp of a doubt, that the Gorgon of Downing Street has a caring nature. It's all in the way the truth is assembled and aimed.'

The truth about what had happened in Wanda's flat could have been humiliating, if it hadn't been presented at the right angle and tilt. As for Sister Meldrum's lesbian affair – Andy had simply listened to other gossip. During his second and third weeks on the ward, he had heard no fewer than five different staff members furtively discussing the matter – though not so furtively that he didn't overhear. June Reilly had deluded herself that she was on to something special, as many over-confident people did. The sad truth – sad, at least, for Sister – was that just about everybody seemed to know.

What Andy had gained, he reckoned, was twofold. For one thing, his own credibility had been strongly reinforced. Secondly, he had established his credentials as a muck-raker. In future, June would be too busy minding her own camouflage to be concerned with penetrating his.

'You're learning, pal, you're learning,' he congratulated himself as he put a cover over the tray. Coming to London may not have been such a bad move after all. Learning to cover his tracks was like playing soccer or squash; the heavier the opposition, the harder he learned to retaliate. All was fair, Andy believed, when it came to shielding his tepid private life. The tactics kept people where they belonged – which was off his back.

9

Debbie had checked the money twice and had come up with two different totals. Neither one agreed with the amount written on the paying-in slip. She looked at the customer, Mr Brothers. He was a funeral director with the stiff, permanently-doleful features of a man who spent more time with the dead than any living soul should. He was staring at her, his drumming fingers signalling his impatience.

'It's not right,' Debbie told him.

'What total do you get?'

'Well, I've counted it twice . . .' She couldn't remember either figure. 'It isn't correct . . .'

'Eight hundred and sixty-three pounds,' Mr Brothers intoned. 'It was precisely right when I handed it across to you.'

'No – '

'Yes.' Mr Brothers flattened both hands on the ledge. 'Count it again, please. Slowly if you don't mind, so I can check it.'

Debbie glanced at the lengthening queue behind the undertaker. There was only one other queue, at Cynthia's till, and it was just as long. People were looking disgruntled.

'Very well,' she snapped.

'And I'll thank you to be more civil.'

Fuming, Debbie flipped through the notes, announcing the sub-totals as she set aside each bundle. At the final count she made it eight hundred and fifty-eight pounds. 'Precisely,' she added, glaring openly at Mr Brothers.

He looked at the neatly stacked money for a moment, pondering. 'How do you think that comes about?'

'I'm not a mindreader, sir.' She saw him inhale sharply. 'At a guess, I'd say you mistook the Scottish fiver for a ten pound note.'

'Give me my receipt, please.'

'You'll have to revise the total on the slip, sir.' Debbie passed back the book. 'And perhaps in future you'll sort the money into denominations, like everyone else does.'

The undertaker's pen stopped halfway through the revision. 'I've never been told I should do that before.'

'It's what you're supposed to do.' He was a very old customer, she knew, and people made concessions. Today there wasn't a concession in her. She watched Mr Brothers complete the new total and took back the book from him. 'Thank you.'

'I wish to see the manager,' he told her as she stamped the counterfoil.

'If you'll tell the receptionist over there, she'll arrange it for you. Next, please.'

The rest of the pre-break period seemed to pass very slowly, an unending parade of dismal people making their dreary transactions. At eleven o'clock Debbie went up to the staff room for coffee. Trudie was on refreshment duty, looking heavily careworn as she struggled to meet the demands of several people at once.

Debbie took her cup to a corner and sat down with it. She took one sip and scowled. 'This is cold!'

'But I've only just made it.' Trudie's forehead took on another little wrinkle. 'Honest.'

Other people looked at each other, then at Debbie.

Their expressions made it clear there was nothing wrong with their coffee.

'I'm telling you it's cold!' The digestive biscuit in Debbie's other hand snapped suddenly, part of it falling to the floor. 'Damn!' She reached down, letting go the other half as she tried to retrieve the fragment on the carpet. As she snatched the whole crumbling lot and sat upright again, her coffee slopped over her knuckles.

'Not your morning, is it?' one of the girls remarked.

Debbie glared at her. 'Mind your own flaming business!' She shot to her feet, dumped the coffee and ruined biscuit on the table and stamped off to the washroom.

Cynthia had witnessed the last few moments as she waited for her cup to be filled. 'What's knotted her knickers this morning?' she demanded of no one in particular.

'Dunno, Cynth,' Trudie sighed. She handed over the coffee. 'She's been in a right mood since she came in.'

'I've noticed.' Cynthia grabbed a couple of biscuits from the tin. She crossed the room and leaned on the wall by the window. 'Old Dowson's on her trail. I don't get the impression he wants to pat her back, either.'

It was at noon, when Debbie handed her till over to another cashier, that the manager beckoned her into his office. She sat down by the polish-smelling desk and watched Mr Dowson arrange his hands before him in a careful tent shape.

'Are there problems?' he asked her at last.

'Problems, Mr Dowson?'

He nodded. 'Problems. You know, difficulties. Troubles. Whatever name comes closest. Do you have any?'

'No, I haven't.'

Dowson sat back. 'You astonish me,' he said, not

84

looking at all astonished. In the opinion of some staff members, his sarcastic mood was his worst. He was inclined to twist the knife more slowly. 'No problems, However do you behave when you *do* have them?'

'I don't understand,' Debbie said.

'Then let me make it clear. This morning you've upset – '

'Oh, him,' she snapped.

The manager leaned forward again, staring at her, making an upturned V of his hands again. 'Is that the way you behave towards customers?'

'Pardon?'

'Do you cut them off before they've finished speaking?'

Debbie stared at her lap. 'I'm sorry.'

'As I was saying, you upset three good and valued customers in the space of ninety minutes.' He sighed delicately. 'The odd, occasional complaint I can understand. I know people can be difficult and sometimes they're entirely in the wrong. But *three*?'

'I don't understand . . .' It was true. She didn't understand. What had she done? She remembered old Mr Brothers and how annoyed he'd looked, but . . .

'Mr Brothers was offended by your brusqueness. Mrs Halliday, never usually one to complain, was more than hurt by the way you told her she was wasting your time by – '

'She'd made out her cheque all wrong . . .'

'You're interrupting again.'

Debbie bit her lip.

'In the case of Mrs Scott, you appear to have set out deliberately to drive a customer to another bank. You told her, did you not, that she might find it more convenient to bank at the Midland?'

Debbie was about to make a firm denial, then she

remembered. The woman had complained, to another woman who was with her, that her daughter received much better attention at the Midland Bank. Debbie had said – not really loudly enough to be heard, she had thought – that the woman should try the other bank, if she wasn't content where she was.

'It was the way she was moaning . . .'

'With more than adequate cause, I imagine.' Mr Dowson slapped one hand quite sharply on the desk. 'Now I ask you again, is there a problem?'

Problem, Debbie thought. *Problem*? Nightmare was the word. 'I – I've not been feeling well.'

'Then perhaps you should see your doctor.' Dowson's voice softened. 'Deborah, how long is it since you sat there and listened to that promising news I had to give you? It seems like ten minutes ago.' He shook his head. 'Now this.'

'I'm very sorry, Mr Dowson.'

'Sorry won't do. If there's any repetition – no, if I have one more complaint about your conduct during the next month, the whole matter will be passed to Regional Head Office for their assessment. Now you know what that could do to your prospects, don't you?'

She nodded. And if she told him what was wrong, she wondered, what damage would that do?

After a short lecture on the necessity to maintain good customer relations at all times, whatever the strain, the manager dismissed Debbie. Back at the till, she adopted a robotic compliance with the rules and kept her mood at a safe distance from the customers.

Towards one o'clock she began to feel a fluttering panic. Would it be safe to go outside? For all she knew he was there – Borrowfield, the barb in her awareness that hurt and hurt and gave her no peace.

Last night had been terrible. It had put her in a state of agitation and misery that had carried over to this morning. It had been responsible for her dressing-down by the manager. The whole thing ran through her mind again as she went for her coat and paused by the window, wondering if she had the courage to go out for an hour.

She had stayed in on her own the night before. She bathed early, put on her nightdress and tried to watch television. The pictures made no sense, the words wouldn't penetrate. By ten she had felt exhausted and decided to go to bed. The telephone in the lounge rang just as she was going into the hall. She answered it offhandedly, sure that the call was for one of the others.

'The blue nightie's perfect,' his voice purred. 'Suits you to a tee. Could do with being a bit shorter, though.'

That was all. He hung up then. He hung up and left Debbie in a state of shuddering terror. She felt both threatened and violated, sick with apprehension as she stood there in the lounge staring through her tears at every closed curtain. It had dawned on her much later, in the early hours of the morning when she still couldn't sleep, that there was an uncurtained window in the passage between the bathroom and the lounge. The explanation brought no peace. He was watching her. The thought was appalling, crushing.

By dawn she was feeling so bad that she even considered telling the others in the flat. But Borrowfield's threat had a strange power of credibility. She'd heard stories of girls who had been raped and battered, treated inhumanly, and still they were subject to leering suspicion. People would rather disbelieve, wouldn't they? It was human nature. They would rather believe that she bore at least *some* of the blame.

She was standing by the bank window, still staring out at the street when Cynthia nudged her. Debbie jumped.

'You look like you could use a drink.' Cynthia took down her own coat and slipped into it. 'Come on, I'll stand you one. The odd liquid lunch doesn't hurt.'

Grateful for the protection of her no-nonsense colleague, Debbie nodded and followed her out across the banking hall.

'One thing,' Cynthia warned as they got to the door.

'What?'

'Don't talk to me about the sports meeting tomorrow. I'm fed up hearing about it.'

Debbie groaned. The sports day. She had forgotten all about it.

Andy approached the bed as the Casualty nurse and the porter moved off with the trolley. The little girl had been propped up on two pillows and tucked in lightly. In Casualty they had washed her and brushed her hair neatly. Even so, she looked devastated.

'Hello,' Andy said. 'I'm Nurse O'Brien. You're Lisa, aren't you?'

The girl looked at her bandaged left arm, touching it shyly. There was a large weal on her forehead and another on her cheek. The knuckles of her right hand were grazed and there was a tube dressing on the thumb.

'How old are you, Lisa?'

She went on gazing at her bandage.

'Let me guess.' Andy pulled up a chair and sat down. 'Now. Let's see. Six? Is that about right?'

The child looked up. Her face was very serious. 'No.'

Andy frowned. 'Not six. Oh dear. I'm not so good at this as I thought. How about . . . How about – nine.'

A smile flickered. 'Nine and a half.'

Andy made a self-deprecating shrug. 'Well I was close, I suppose. 'I'll have to get in more practice.' He smiled and touched Lisa's shoulder. 'What would you like to drink? We've got orange, lemonade, Coke . . .'

He stopped and turned as a man approached. He was tall and silver-haired, with a strong face and thick dark eyebrows. He carried a black attaché case.

'Staff Nurse O'Brien?'

Andy stood up. 'That's right.'

'I was told you're in charge. I'm Dr Legg – I do one day a week here, in Cardiology.' He nodded towards the bed. 'The girl's one of the patients from my general practice.'

'Oh, I see. Would you like to have a word with her, Doctor?'

'Just a quick one. Then if I might have speak with you for a minute . . .'

'Of course.' Andy turned to the child. 'Will I make it a Coke?'

She nodded, a sharp, single movement of her head.

'Right. I'll be back with it when you've had time to talk to your visitor.'

Dr Legg took the vacated chair and smiled broadly at the girl. 'Remember me, Lisa? I gave you all those nasty vaccinations. And I saw to you when you had measles, and when you had a bad throat about a year ago. Remember?' When she nodded and began fingering her bandage again he drew the chair closer to the bed. 'I heard what happened to you, Lisa. We're going to see it doesn't happen again.'

Without looking up she said, 'Where's my mum?'

'She's at home, love, but she'll be along to see you soon.' He looked round the ward briefly. 'You'll find a lot of new pals in here, by the look of it.' He reached out

89

and touched her shoulder as Andy had done. 'You'll like it in this place. They're all very kind and they'll see no harm comes to you. Just tell them if there's anything you want and I'm sure they'll get you it, if they can.'

He stood up as Andy brought the drink. Lisa took the cup carefully. 'Ta,' she murmured.

'It's a pleasure, madam.' Andy winked at her. 'See you in a few minutes.'

Dr Legg went with Andy to the office. They sat down and exchanged serious looks.

'Five more minutes, I understand,' Andy said, 'and she might have been dead. As it was, she started screaming blue murder as soon as he grabbed her. But he got in a few damaging punches.'

'The family has a history of child abuse. There's an older boy, fifteen now, who took a few rough knocks. Nothing was proved, but it was clear enough what had happened. It's all down to the father, mind you. The mother's only a passive accomplice. She won't report him and she tries to cover up. This time I gather she caught some of the punishment herself.'

'She tried to stop him hitting the girl. It was a neighbour who raised the alarm.' Andy shook his head. 'I still don't understand how they can do these things to their children.'

Dr Legg shrugged. 'He was drunk . . .'

'Drunk or not.'

'It's the pattern, though. Unemployed, no prospects, he gets drunk to smother the boredom and the feeling of uselessness. Then the drink releases the pent-up anger . . .'

'And he batters a defenceless child.'

Dr Legg frowned. 'The youngster's dependence on him creates part of the frustration. The child's needs underline his inadequacy, the poor little creature's a focus for what boils up . . .'

Andy folded his arms and stared at the window.

'I take it,' Dr Legg said cautiously, 'that you don't hold with that explanation. I have to admit it's leaky.'

'Very.'

'But it's persuasive. My practice is in Albert Square. I see a lot of the harsher offshoots of unemployment and deprivation.' Dr Legg gestured with his hand, a little helplessly. 'You probably see a great deal more of this kind of thing than I do. Forgive me for preaching.'

'Not at all,' Andy said gruffly. 'Lately, I've been prompted to take the very same point of view you were expressing. But I was offered the other one, too.'

Dr Legg nodded. 'The shiftless society. Survival's too easy. Is that the point of view you mean?'

'That's it. They don't have to struggle. They explore only what's within easy reach. It softens them till they go bad.' He paused. 'I have to say, though, that I haven't adopted either view yet.'

For a moment Dr Legg looked thoughtful. 'The truly aimless population's out there, certainly,' he said. 'But I can't help thinking there are others, worthy people, badly damaged by the loss of natural rights – and I think there are more of that kind than the other . . .' He stopped abruptly and slapped both hands on his knees. 'This isn't the time to discuss the plight of modern man, is it? I just wanted to say something about young Lisa out there.'

'Of course.'

'It's about her future safety. This is the second time she's been attacked, and this time it can be proved that her father is the culprit. There are outside witnesses. But. If the facts of what happened are in any way understated – '

'They might send her back home.'

The doctor nodded. 'And I think that would be a bad thing, for the present anyway. On paper, the child suffered a few bruises, a severely twisted knee, some minor cuts and that's about all. The same could happen to her in any boisterous outdoor game. When the social workers and police come round I don't want you to exaggerate anything, but . . .'

Andy nodded. 'I've a lot of experience at making them understand where the real damage is done,' he assured him. 'Don't worry.'

'Thank you.' Dr Legg stood up. 'I'll leave you to get on, then.'

They walked together to the ward entrance. On the way Dr Legg asked Andy how long he had been away from Scotland. When Andy told him the doctor looked surprised.

'The softness of your accent suggests you've been down here longer.'

'I was a foster child. I came under a variety of influences, and I lived with about as many varieties of Lowland dialect.'

As they paused by the entrance Dr Legg jerked his thumb back at the ward. 'Young Lisa might end up being fostered, mightn't she? Do you recommend it?'

'I don't think it did me any harm,' Andy said. 'It makes you a bit detached, perhaps, but that's probably not a bad thing. In Lisa's case, I'm sure being fostered would be a big improvement on living at home.'

'Hear, hear.' Dr Legg began to move off, then he hesitated. 'What we were talking about – you know, the reasons for all this brutality and lawlessness, the cruelty to children in particular – do you feel you do tend towards one theory for its cause?'

'Well . . .' Andy frowned.

'I ask,' Dr Legg said, 'because I'm interested to know the reaction of a man who works with so many child victims. I like to hear all shades of well-informed opinion.' He smiled. 'You might call it a trick to stop my own point of view from getting too fixed.'

'My view changes from day to day,' Andy confessed. 'But on balance, most times I'd like to lay unfriendly hands on the ones who do it to kids.'

The doctor nodded. 'I understand.' He moved off a few paces and turned. 'How do you cope with it?'

'With what?'

'The daily kindling of the aggressive impulse.'

'Sport,' Andy said firmly. 'It's amazing how accurate your technique gets when you imagine a ball is somebody's head.'

The doctor smiled. 'Maybe a lot more people should take up games,' he said, waving as he walked away.

10

'Would you just look at that stupid little twonk,' Nosher Brent said. 'Struttin' about like he was in the bleedin' Gestapo.'

Nosher, a russet-cheeked hospital porter nicknamed because of his enormous stomach – which was really a beer gut – was clad in an outsize white tee shirt, baggy navy shorts, red knee socks and old-style football boots. He stood with hands on hips, belly jutting, surrounded by the other members of the hospitals' five-a-side team, who were clad in more conventional soccer gear.

'It's likely the only chance he's ever had to tell anybody to do anything,' Andy O'Brien pointed out. 'The poor soul's enjoying himself.'

'He'll get two or three studs up his ring piece if he tries tellin' *me* what to do,' Nosher growled. 'See if he don't.'

The meeting was being held in a large, roped-off section of Hurlingham Park, in Fulham. The site had been acquired for the day by the object of Nosher's ridicule, a young, oily-haired bank official wearing a brand new St Michael track suit and pink trainers. He appeared to have been rewarded for his bargaining skill by being given the biggest cardboard badge with STEWARD printed on it, plus the superficial authority that went with the title.

'I was watchin' the girls' relay team, meself.' The other porter on the team, Gil Raymond, had the looks and bearing of a youngish dockside Greek. Women were inclined to like him until he spoke. 'See that one down on the end there?' He pointed to the string of girls twenty yards away. They were in shorts and shirts with numbers tacked to their backs. 'Her in the blue an' red. See her? I reckon I give her one, once.'

'You don't half talk a load of cobblers,' Nosher said. The familiarity was surprising, since the two men worked at different hospitals and had met only that afternoon. 'How would the likes of you get within touchin' distance of the likes of her?'

'You'd be surprised, mate,' Gil said, his voice throaty, one eyelid drooping for a second. 'Them middle-class ones, they like a bit of skilled handlin'. The good lookin' ones especially.'

Nosher spat. 'She wouldn't let you touch her with a barge-pole's barge-pole.'

'I know different,' Gil said, 'don't I?'

'Cobblers!'

'An' bollocks to you!'

Andy and the two other members of the team, his flatmate Geoff Mercer and a junior surgeon called Perry Long who worked at Islington General, were easing themselves away from the porters' slanging match. They huddled by a tree eight feet away and Geoff leaned his head against it.

'I shouldn't have come here,' he groaned. 'My head feels like it's been belted with a gas cooker.'

'Serves you right,' Andy said.

'Aah, don't be so smug. Just because you can't hold your drink . . .'

'You're the one that can't hold it, China. I mean look at you . . .'

'All right. all right.' Geoff waved an arm for peace. 'That barney going on over there's quite enough without us having one of our own.' He raised his head and appealed to Perry with his eyes.

'I told you already,' Perry said, 'I haven't got anything on me.'

'Christ.' Geoff rolled his eyes. 'Every junior doc I've met carries some kind of uppers. You don't have to go respectable until you're a Registrar, you know. Didn't anybody tell you?'

Perry looked at his watch. 'What time are we supposed to start?'

Andy shrugged. 'After the ladies' relay, I think.'

'By the time they sort themselves out, I'll have gone terminal,' Geoff groaned. He shuffled away from the tree. 'Hey, Nosher. What's good for a hangover?'

'You're a nurse,' Andy pointed out. 'You're supposed to know about these things.'

'This is folk medicine,' Geoff said. 'I'm asking one of the folk.'

Nosher swung his stomach in Geoff's direction. 'Hangover? Bad, is it?'

'Terrible.'

'Well.' Nosher scratched his nose. 'Best thing I know is the juice of two bottles of Guinness.'

Geoff turned back to the other two. 'Right. If I'm going to be dragging my ailing giblets round that pitch for twenty minutes, we're going to need some strategy. What kind of talent's on the other side?'

'That's them.' Perry pointed to five strapping young men in football shirts bearing the bank's logo. They were chatting to the hospitals' ladies' running team.

'They look kind of healthy,' Perry observed.

Geoff nodded grimly. 'Right. They're big, so probably they're hard and no doubt they're fast.'

The other two nodded.

'So what kind of tactics do you suggest?' Perry enquired dryly.

'When I was in my school team,' Geoff said, 'we had an emergency technique when we came up against something like that.'

'What did you do?'

'We kicked the shit out of them.'

Two hundred yards away, in her neatly pressed pink shirt and running shorts – which weren't quite so brief as the other girls' – Debbie was standing alone, gazing across towards the brightly-painted houses beyond the park, on Hurlingham Road. It was a nice day, she was telling herself. A warm, balmy afternoon with all the freshness of spring in the breeze.

'Fresh and bright and lovely,' she whispered.

As a child, whenever she was bored or fed up, she had often done that; she would stand at the window or in the yard outside and tell herself she was lucky to exist in such a pretty world. It was odd that the trick usually worked in the grubby surroundings where she grew up, yet in this wide, leafy, fragrant parkland it didn't work at all.

She turned and stared at the bustle of competitors in their rainbow colours, all milling around making excited noises. Everybody appeared to be smiling or laughing. It was an occasion devised more for fun, Debbie knew, than to prove anything special about athletic talents. It all looked foreign to her, she realized, because it was completely alien to her mood.

'Come on then, Debbie.' The young man with STEWARD on his chest was beckoning with his clipboard. 'You're first leg in the relay. Time to line up.'

She would have liked to crack his clipboard over his greasy head. Instead, she walked across to the start of the running track, marked off in an oval with fluttering, rope-linked pennants.

She took her place automatically. She could feel the

tension in the girl beside her. Debbie wasn't feeling the least bit enthusiastic or keyed-up. All she had to do, after all, was run a few yards with a baton, pass it on, and that was that. Big deal.

From his vantage point on the gentle rise beyond the five-a-side pitch, Andy stood with the other four and watched as the starter fired his pistol. The two girls streaked away from the start, batons gripped, legs pumping, feet throwing up tracers of dust.

'The one in the pink can move,' Andy murmured.

'I like pink on a girl,' Gil said distantly.

Perry shook his head. 'She's the bank's girl. Look at ours.'

'Draggin' her arse a bit,' Nosher observed. 'She's bound to be a ward orderly.'

The bank team's baton was passed-on a clear second ahead of the other. On the second leg the gap widened. By that time, Andy had stopped following the event. He was watching the girl in the pink shirt. As soon as she'd passed on the baton she had walked away from the race without looking back. There was something touchingly solitary about her, he thought.

The bank won the ladies' relay. The five-a-side team were still watching the jubilant little crowd round the finish line when the young man with the big badge appeared a few yards to their left. He emitted a piercing whistle and pointed at the play area.

Nosher turned and glared at him. 'Is he whistlin' at us, d'you reckon?'

The steward whistled again and beckoned them imperiously towards the pitch, where the bank's team were already lining up.

It was clear that the steward was a stickler for his timetable. As the hospitals' team began ambling towards the pitch, he whistled a third time, his arm waving like a traffic policeman's. Nosher took a detour to confront him.

'What's with all the whistlin', Titch? Lost your dog or somethin'?'

The steward gazed up over the mound of Nosher's belly. 'It's time to start the five-a-side,' he snapped.

'Whistle at me one more time, sonny, an' you'll end up on the deck with a chalk line round you.'

A crowd of spectators gathered along the perimeter of the pitch as the two teams faced each other. The bank's players looked even more formidable in close-up. Perry said as much.

'Bunch of fairies,' Nosher growled.

Andy glanced at Geoff. He had the stoical expression of a doomed but determined warrior. On his other side Gil was throwing a provocative sneer at the opposition. Perry simply looked ready.

The whistle went and Andy found himself, instantly, in the exhilarated state that only sport induced in him. He was at one with his body. Mind and muscle linked with sinew and skill and drove him towards a single, clear objective. Somewhere to his right he heard Nosher roar a terrible warning at his enemies as the teams thundered into the conflict.

Twenty minutes later, both sides lay littered about the pitch, panting, some of them groaning, a very few laughing as they guzzled cold drinks. Leaning on the perimeter rope, the referee quietly remarked to a shocked spectator that it had been a massacre.

'Or the closest to one I hope I'll ever see.'

'It was shocking,' the spectator said. He was a bank inspector by profession, a man used to measured, civilized exchanges. 'That hospital bunch are no better than brutes. Savages.'

The referee nodded. 'They won, though, didn't they?'

The view taken by the supporters of the East London Hospitals was that their team, heavily outclassed, had used nothing short of genius to even the balance. All were agreed that Andy was the one true footballer of the five, and he scored the three goals. But he would never have managed without his guerrillas.

'A game to remember, lads,' Gil remarked, spilling 7-Up down his shirt. 'Talk about mid-field supremacy, eh? We pissed all over them.'

Elbows, knees, Gil's forehead and Nosher's belly had cut a swathe through the opposition's unexpectedly chivalrous attack. Even Perry, a mild man off the pitch, had used his slight weight to advantage by hurling it at full force, several times and without fear, into the chests of oncoming opponents. All straightforward fouling was kept to the referee's blind side. All blatant outrages were committed behind his back. The net result was a three-nil victory, with a few injuries on the bank's side.

'That'll show the bastards,' Nosher wheezed as he lolled on the grass beside Andy. 'All I kept thinkin' was, "the sods work for a bank." I hate banks.' He finished his soft drink and squashed the can. 'Reckon I'll go over the beer tent an' get plastered now. Lovely finish to a lovely day. What about you?'

'I've got the long-jump yet,' Andy sighed.

Nosher tutted. 'Quit while you're winnin', that's what I say.' He belched softly. 'You can take sport too seriously, you know.'

Half an hour later, following the men's and then the women's three-hundred metres, Andy found himself watching the girl in the pink shirt again. She had come

100

second in her race. Immediately after, as she had done in the relay, she simply walked away. She behaved as if she had been a fleeting interloper, no part of the unified gaggle of competitors. He saw her stand in her curious solitude, gazing out across the park.

Later still when Andy, to his surprise, had won the men's long jump, he sat on the grass and watched the little one in pink line herself up for the same event. She didn't appear to be nervous. In fact she looked unnaturally calm. Andy had seen calm competitors before, dispassionate to the point of indifference; she was like that, but there was something more. It was as if she was engaged on one thing while all her concentration was somewhere else.

She won. Tradition demanded that the male and female winners pose together for a photograph. As Andy stood awkwardly beside her, waiting for the photographer to line up his shot, he murmured his congratulations.

'Thanks,' she said, without smiling. 'Same to you.'

Definitely an absent spirit, he decided. As soon as the pictures had been taken she was off on her own again, strolling away across the grass. Andy stood mopping his neck with a towel, using the action to cover the fact he was still watching her. After a moment Geoff Mercer sidled up.

'Coming for a drink, champ?'

Andy took a last glance at the girl. Her name, he had gathered, was Debbie. It fitted her. He looked at Geoff. 'Give me time to get my track suit on and I'll be right with you,' he said.

The atmosphere inside the beer tent was the same as the body-warm, smoky fug in any overcrowded public bar, except that the light was better. Armed with pints, Andy and Geoff squeezed through the crowd and found

Nosher and Gil. They were leaning on opposite sides of a support post, arguing again.

'You're only obsessed with crumpet because you're not gettin' enough,' Nosher barked.

'An' you put it down 'cause you can't manage.'

They had enough mutual belligerence, Andy thought, to make them lifelong friends.

'What do you reckon?' Nosher appealed to Geoff. 'This character reckons he can turn women on just by lookin' at them.'

'In the right way,' Gil interjected. 'There's a knack to it.'

'An I say,' Nosher went on, 'that he's got nookie on the noodle. Can't talk about nothin' else, an' he's full of all this crap about technique an' style an' how they can hardly keep their hands off him. Crumpet starvation, that's his trouble. It's warped his view of life. What do you reckon?'

Geoff shrugged. 'I can't make a diagnosis without more case details.'

Nosher took a gulp from his glass and stared disdainfully at Gil, who was leering sidelong at a girl by the bar. 'Whatever you've got, mate, you want to get it sorted out before it sends you off your nut. An' try gettin' women into proportion while you're at it.'

'You reckon?' Gil said, grinning.

'Yeah. Now me, I know I'm safer stayin' obsessed with this.' Nosher tapped his beer glass. 'I've never forgot me grandad's warnin'. He told me that pussy an' gunpowder's the two most dangerous things in the world.'

As Perry joined them Andy glanced aside, idly scanning the faces in the tent. There were a few he knew, but most of the crowd were bank people. He wondered, not at all seriously, if he and his companions might suddenly find themselves ambushed by a gang of revenge-hungry clerks.

Suddenly he was staring. Beyond the back flap of the tent, which had been folded aside to let out the smoke, he saw the girl in pink again. Debbie. She was by a perimeter rope about fifteen yards away. She wasn't alone any longer. There was a man with her, tall and smartly dressed. He was standing close to Debbie; her back was touching the rope. His lips were moving steadily and his expression was casual. But Debbie's expression wasn't casual. It wasn't remote as it had been before, either. Andy knew he could be reading things all wrong, but he believed the girl looked frightened.

'I'll be back in a minute,' he said. The others were into some new discussion and didn't take any notice.

Andy edged his way through the crush until he was beside the open flap. He paused and checked. The man had a grip on Debbie's arm now. He still looked pretty calm and he was still doing all the talking. Debbie, for her part, still looked distressed.

Andy stepped outside the tent. He tried for a casual air, taking steady sips from his glass, pausing to sniff the air and gaze across the grassy acreage. Moving as slowly as his anxiety would let him, he took a ziz-zagging route across the space between the tent and the perimeter rope. There were a few other people in the area, legitimate casual strollers, none of them very close to where Debbie and the man were standing. Andy got as near as he could, without making himself conspicuous. He stood with his back to the couple, pretending to drink, listening hard.

' . . . Wouldn't want that kind of upset anyway, would you?' he heard the man say.

Debbie's voice wavered when she spoke. 'There's a law to protect me – '

'Debbie, Debbie . . . All this talk about law, the police and the rest. It's nonsense. Unnecessary . . .'

'You act like you're normal. But you're not. What normal person would – '

'You misunderstand.'

'I'll tell somebody. I will!' The squeaking tail-off of her voice made Andy's neck-hair prickle.

'We've been through all that,' the man said. 'If you'd simply let me prove . . .' A gust of wind drowned the rest. What Andy heard next was a distinct, alarming whimper from Debbie.

He turned, watching over the rim of his glass. The man had both hands on her now. She was beginning to squirm.

'I won't stop you running,' he said, smiling. 'But I'll be there, Debbie. Always there. Why try to get away from what's inevitable?'

To Andy the man looked deranged. He had seen that serene craziness before, the whole awful truth of the matter visible nowhere but in the eyes.

'You've got to stop this!' Debbie howled weakly. 'You're wrecking my *life*!'

Andy dropped the glass and strode forward. When he was two paces away the man saw him. His hands dropped away from Debbie's arms as he glared at Andy.

'Having trouble are you, Debbie?' Andy kept his voice light, his eyes on the man.

Debbie stared at him and gulped, catching her breath.

'Why don't you run along and mind your own petty business, sonny?'

Andy stepped close. 'Sonny, did you say?'

The unhinged look was withdrawing from the man's

eyes. Plain anger was taking its place. 'That's right. *Sonny*. Go and play rounders with your pals.'

Debbie was backing away.

'Listen,' Andy said. He put his face close to the man's. 'I don't know what this is about, but you were getting pretty heavy with my friend here . . .'

'Friend?' The man made a wild, exaggerated grin. 'She's not your – '

'He is my friend,' Debbie said. Her voice still wavered.

'Well it's no business of yours, friend – '

'I'm sticking my nose in, anyway.'

'Push off!' The man slapped a hand on Andy's chest and shoved.

What happened next was something Andy could describe and demonstrate, but was rarely able to teach anyone, even people who badly wanted to learn. It was known among a few lads in Glasgow as Andy's Mr Spock move. Technically, his right hand made swift contact with the man's left shoulder; his thumb pressed firmly forward on the sternocleidomastoid muscle, while his fingers squeezed inwards on the lower end of the splenius capitis muscle at the back of the neck, trapping a cervical nerve. To Debbie, it looked as if he simply touched the man's shoulder.

'Ow!' The man landed heavily on his knees, clutching his neck. 'You bastard!'

Andy bent low by the contorted face. 'I think you should do the pushing off, pal, while you're still able.' He had deliberately thickened the Glasgow accent. 'Before you go, I'll warn you to keep away from Debbie. I know who you are and I know where you live. If you don't behave, you'll find out the real harm I can do you.'

The man scrambled to his feet. For a moment he stared

at Andy. All that showed now in his eyes was an impotent, childlike defiance.

'On your bike,' Andy snarled.

'Listen you, I've a good mind to – '

'Whatever you do to me,' Andy said quietly, 'I'll let you have back. Tenfold.'

The man threw an unsteady glance at Debbie then ducked under the rope. He strode off towards the parking area, still rubbing his neck.

Andy turned to Debbie. She was standing with her hands hugging her elbows, seeming much smaller than before. She was pale and cold looking.

'I hope you didn't think that was an intrusion,' Andy said. 'It looked like an emergency, or I wouldn't have interfered . . .'

'You didn't intrude. I'm very grateful.' She didn't seem capable of movement.

'Come on.' Andy guided her by the elbow, feeling as if he were dealing with one of his young patients. 'I'll get you a drink. I think you've got a touch of shock.'

The crowd in the tent had thinned. Andy positioned Debbie in a corner then went to the bar and got her a brandy. She thanked him and sipped it cautiously.

In the aftermath, Andy began to feel a little awkward. He gulped his fresh glass of beer, watching Debbie make her dainty way through the brandy. After a minute's silence, she looked up at him.

'Do you really know him?' she asked.

Andy smiled. 'No. Never saw him in my life before. But I've seen his type.'

'So all that about knowing where he lived and getting back at him . . .'

'Glasgow hard-man patter. Deterrent talk.'

'What was the other thing? Karate?'

'A variation. Strictly for self-defence.'

Another minute passed. Andy cleared his throat. 'Well . . .' He shuffled his feet and looked at the puddle in the bottom of his glass. Then he looked at Debbie. 'Are you going to be all right?'

'Yes, I think so.' She made a little smile. 'I'm afraid I forgot your name. I heard it earlier, but – '

'Andy. Andy O'Brien.'

'I'm very, very grateful, Andy.'

The strong intent in Andy, which he had been trying to ignore, flared suddenly into action. 'You're in a wee bit of a state, Debbie. Could I suggest a meal afterwards, or something . . .' He read her face, wishing he hadn't said it. She was frowning at him. 'I just thought, to help shake off what happened . . .'

'It's nice of you, but . . .'

'That's all right,' he said quickly. 'As I said, I just thought . . .' He gestured with the empty glass. 'If you're sure you're OK, I'll go and catch up with the lads.' He felt the damnable blush. It made him want to get away as fast as he could. He began sidling to the entrance. 'Nice to meet you, Debbie.' He turned away sharply.

'Andy.'

'Mm?' He turned back to her and noticed, to his surprise, that she was blushing, too. He hadn't seen a girl blush in years.

She smiled again. 'I didn't say no.'

'Pardon?'

'I couldn't face dinner, not the way I'm feeling. That's what I was going to say. But a drink somewhere would be nice.'

God Almighty, he thought. *God Almighty*!

'I think I owe you a bottle of wine at least, for your kindness.' Her blush deepened.

Andy was beguiled. In her charming awkwardness he saw a timidity that mirrored his own. Staring at her, he realized he was expected to say something.

'That's – that's great, Debbie. Smashing. Is there anywhere special you'd like to go?'

11

The smoky, low-ceilinged chamber appeared to have been designed for posing. Strategically-placed spotlights pierced the dark amber light with shafts of red, blue and yellow, spreading in cones to highlight and silhouette hairdos and smart clothes. Those standing near the bar could move their heads this way and that, creating precisely the desired dramatic effects – which could be checked in the mirrors hung on the glazed-brick walls. Even the less vain of the clientele, sitting at tables scattered about the remaining floor space, could rest assured that the tinted gloom did the most for their complexions.

'I suppose it's a bit twee,' Debbie said, 'but they're not a rowdy bunch.' They were at a table near the centre of the room, surrounded by low-murmuring couples and the occasional, wistfully-solo male. 'There's never any trouble in this place.'

Andy could believe that. Nobody in a thirty-quid Sergio Savarin jacket and designer jeans was going to risk getting their gear damaged or their hairstyle wrecked. Safer to stick with your own kind.

'How often do you come here?' he asked.

'Just often enough to be called a regular,' she said, then added hastily, 'Never on my own, of course. Although some girls do.'

Andy sensed her disapproval of any woman who would do a thing like that. He had never felt safer with a girl in all his life. In his memory there was a collection of old, scary encounters, dating from the time he was seventeen. Among them were memories of a few girls who had made him feel safe enough, girls who, just for once, had seemed not to be expecting more than his company. But they had always come up with the challenge, sooner or later, and he had always fled. None of those girls, in his recollection, had ever been like Debbie.

'They're nice people who run the place. French, I think, although one of my flatmates said she thought they were Belgian.'

That was the kind of conversation they had restricted themselves to, so far. He'd given her a summary of his background and his job, she had obliged him with the same. Tastes in music had been touched upon, so had likes and dislikes in television shows and films. No mention, so far, of what had brought them here.

Andy tilted back the wine bottle and read the label: *Niersteiner Gutes Domtal*. 'This is nice,' he said. He had drunk two glasses. So had Debbie. The flowery flavour was surprisingly unsweet as it hit the palate. It also gave him the sort of glow he liked best – slow dawning, with no threat of sudden, onrushing intoxication. He felt he could drink it all night.

'It's one of their better wines,' Debbie said. She had insisted on buying it, in spite of Andy's strenuous protests. 'There's nothing nicer than good wine, is there? In moderation, of course.'

The juke box was playing a Donna Summer track. Andy tapped the table lightly, matching the beat, finding it easy to sit there without saying much. There was no pressure on him. Debbie appeared to be in the same state, though she was still, perhaps, a little nervous.

'It's been a funny old day,' she said suddenly.

At last, Andy thought. So far, she had behaved as if

110

this was just a pleasant, ordinary date, rather than the therapeutic follow-up to a horrendous experience.

'You can say that again.' He watched her finger the foot of her glass, nudging it in a jerky circle on the shiny table top. 'It's none of my business, of course, Debbie . . .'

'I don't mind talking about it,' she said. Her eyes flicked across his. 'It would be a relief, actually. But I don't want to bore you . . .'

'You wouldn't be doing that.'

His memory flashed. The girl in pink; her touching solitariness; the odd, near-tingle in his stomach as he had watched her. Now she was here, alone with him, and she was prepared to unburden herself. He felt a measure of bliss. And gratitude.

He stood up. 'Before we go any further,' he said, responding to a wise impulse, 'I'll get us another bottle.' There were still two glassfuls unpoured, but he didn't want a sudden break-off in her flow just because they'd run out of wine. 'I'll take this one with me, to show them the label. I don't think I could get my mouth round the name.'

When they were settled with the two bottles beside them, Andy put his elbows on the table. Debbie took a gulp of wine, put down the glass and sighed.

'Well. It started a while ago. It seems like an age.'

It took her fifteen minutes to tell him. From time to time, as it became easier to talk, she would pause in the account to describe her feelings at a particular moment in her ordeal. She told him about her near-hysteria and about the sense of being violated and persecuted. At the end of the tale Andy had an impression of a girl driven to the limits of her endurance, yet still able to carry on

111

with her daily life. He suspected that Debbie had more emotional resilience than she knew.

'I'll tell you something that might surprise you,' Andy said when she had finished. He topped the glasses, noting that they had almost finished the second bottle. 'That man's behaviour isn't very rare.'

She stared at him. 'I've been pestered before, Andy. But this wasn't the same. Nothing like it. There was something . . .'

'Sick. It's a sickness with a name.'

'Really?'

'Oh yes.' Andy felt a strong urge to air his professional insight. Studying abnormal psychology had been almost a hobby during his later training; he had suspected, once or twice, that he was checking himself out. 'In this case it's a cocktail ailment with quite a few ingredients.'

'What's it called, then?'

'Basically, what this character suffers from is called an Obsessive-Compulsive Neurosis.'

'Gosh.'

The inclination to show off was nearly irresistible. Debbie, after all, was being offered an explanation of what had been inflicted on her. That was powerful stuff. She was hooked, a captive listener. Even so, Andy curbed the temptation to run off at the mouth with high-sounding jargon and cute analysis. He tried, instead, for a straight-forward explanation.

'You have to be careful not to confuse an ordinary pest with somebody who's got this disorder,' he said. 'A pest will be put off when he realizes he doesn't stand a chance. The obsessive-compulsive type, on the other hand, *must* succeed. He believes his whole future wellbeing depends on it. If he doesn't succeed, something bad will happen to him, or so he thinks.'

'And what you did – hurting him and threatening him – will that put him off?'

'Probably,' Andy said. 'See, he's failed in the task he set himself, hasn't he? Before he could get you to give in, the bad thing happened. He got a very sore neck and a Gorbals curse thrown in for good measure. So the prophesy was fulfilled.'

'But won't he just do it all over again, with somebody else?'

Andy nodded. 'It's likely. He needs treatment. His madness, if you care to call it that, needs dismantling – though by the look of him, that would take a lot of work. His condition's well established.'

'How can you tell?'

'They usually start small. Making themselves steal from shops, stuff like that.'

Debbie nodded, but she was frowning. 'I'm sure what you say is right – but there was something more about him. Something – well, the way he looked, it was like he was, you know . . .' Her hands fluttered for a moment. 'Those sex killers you hear about, I can imagine they look the way he did.'

'That's why I said it's a cocktail ailment.' Andy hesitated even to name the other disorders that could be part of Borrowfield's sickness; they were all a shade too embarrassing to talk about. He contented himself by explaining, almost apologetically, that the man's sex-drive was inflated and off-focus.

Debbie raised her glass to her lips. 'Everything's wrapped up with sex nowadays,' she said, then swallowed the wine.

Andy nodded. To some people, her remark might have sounded prudish. To him, it was further reassurance. This was his idea of a good girl.

He checked the time. The wine was buzzing round his veins now, pleasantly softening him. Even so, the temptation to drink more might lead to a loss of control, however small. He wanted to stay in charge of himself tonight.

'How do you feel about eating now, Debbie?'

'Well.' She looked down; when she looked up again she was smiling. 'To tell you the truth, I'm famished.'

They went to a Chinese restaurant on Wandsworth High Street. Over the main course Debbie began to talk about the coincidence of her coming from Walford and Andy actually working there.

'Odd, isn't it? A lot of important events in my life have had strong coincidences attached to them.'

Did she mean, Andy wondered, that meeting him was an important event? It was more likely she meant that the rescue was important.

'Yes,' he said, 'coincidence is strange.'

If he'd had the courage, he would have told her of a really strange coincidence. The very girl who had caught his attention at the sports meeting was the same one he was with now, dining with her and enjoying himself more than he had in a long time. Furthermore, if he hadn't been watching her all afternoon, he would never have saved her bacon and they wouldn't be here together.

'The man who first interviewed me from the bank, for instance,' Debbie went on. 'He had the same surname as me. My birth date is the same as my supervisor's. And I once had a boyfriend whose mother's maiden name was the same as *my* mother's.'

'Amazing,' Andy murmured. Boyfriend, he thought. Had there been many? Was this evening a one-off? Good girls probably played safe by never getting too deeply involved. Short relationships and one-time-only dates could be a guaranteed way to keep life uncomplicated.

With the wine still singing lightly in him, Andy ventured the kind of question he wouldn't have asked when he was sober. 'Do you have a lot of boyfriends, Debbie?'

Interestingly, she blushed. Only a little. As she concentrated on spooning some prawns from the hot tray on to her plate, she murmured. 'Well, no.' When she had completed the transfer she looked up. 'How about you?'

'No,' he grinned. 'No boyfriends at all.'

Debbie laughed. 'But seriously. You work with females all the time, you're bound to have a lot of friends among them.'

'No, I don't,' Andy said. 'Nobody who's close, anyway.' Maybe it was bad for his image to tell her that, but he felt it was right to level with her. 'There are a lot of men in your business, aren't there?'

'Point taken.' Debbie made a sour face. 'It's hard to think of *them* as men.'

When the meal was over and the waiter brought coffee, Debbie sank back in her chair and grinned at Andy.

'I can't begin to tell you . . .' She let out a contented sigh.

'What? Try.'

'It's just such a – a huge relief. I can still hardly believe it. When this day started, I never thought I'd smile again. And now look. All that worry's been lifted off me, and as if that wasn't enough, I've had a lovely evening. Thanks to you.'

'It hasn't all been one-sided.'

For the brief instant that her face was still, Andy registered every detail; the eyes, bright and clear with a catlike set, the generous mouth parted to show fine even teeth, the luxuriant fair hair saved from wildness by her

115

centre parting. Every detail was attractive to him, the total effect compelling. *Will I see her again*?

When they left the restaurant they walked back slowly to where Debbie lived. At the front steps she paused and looked up at him.

'Thanks again, Andy. It's been very nice.'

Questions tumbled. Did she find him special? If so, was it him, or was it what he had done for her? He heard his feet shift on the pavement.

'Best Saturday night I've had in ages,' he said.

'Same here.'

Endearingly, more so than she could know, she held out her hand. Andy shook it gently. Its warmth felt amazingly intimate. He believed she was hesitating. Or did he imagine it? He who hesitates . . .

'Could I maybe see you again?' he mumbled.

She nodded at once. 'If you want.'

Great! he thought. 'Well, maybe we should work out a time. I work some evenings – '

'And I'm starting night classes again . . .' She held up a finger briefly, like a teacher about to scold a child. 'Tell you what.' She opened her bag, took out a little spiral-backed notebook and a pen. She scribbled on a page, tore it out and gave it to Andy. 'That's my work number, the one underneath's the flat. Give me a ring when you know your timetable and we'll work something out.'

'Great.' He pocketed the slip. 'See you soon, then.'

'See you, Andy.'

She clip-clopped up the steps and waved to him at the top. He waved back, turned, and walked off like a king. A few minutes later it didn't bother him at all to discover that, once again, he was lost.

12

The passing of a single year, with all its upheavals, its small felicities and setbacks and hard-won advances, had left Andy's professional life unaltered. Even the big event of the year left no mark of change. The Nurses' Day of Action was a one-day national strike designed to show the government – and the people – how strongly the profession felt about being paid, as well as treated, like minor scullions. The event did no more than prove, Dr Norris remarked, that the Iron Lady and her tin men would never make any move that might encourage people to believe they lived in a democracy.

Andy's private life, on the other hand, was changed so wondrously that, even a year after meeting Debbie, he would wake up some mornings and wonder if he had dreamt it all. After so long on the outside, he was now able to strut with the best of them. He no longer had to bend the truth and make excuses. There were no more panics in one-to-one situations with women, either, because he had nothing to prove; could back down from any advances without loss of face – he was, after all, one half of a couple.

Professionally, Debbie's life had undergone a change. With one more certificate gained and rolled up safely in her woolly-jumper drawer, she had been entrusted with a post in the Securities Department. It was an advance in one sense, a reversal in another; she was back to being the junior member on the team, surrounded by people of senior rank and experience who never let her forget the fact. Her sense of direction remained strong, though; a place in management was still her goal, and when, sometimes, the going seemed very rough, she reminded herself that anything worthwhile was never easily won.

She drew great consolation from her private life. She had known from the first that Andy, if not destined to be her man, was certainly her kind of man. There had always been a Woman's Own simplicity to her notion of the ideal partner. The bell had rung loud and sharp as she sat there in the wine bar taking furtive stock. The ideal chap had to be quiet-mannered, intelligent and witty, without being brash. Andy scored heavily there. He also had to be tall and handsome – dark was optional, but Andy incorporated that bonus, anyway. In addition, it was terribly important that the man in her life would show her great respect. Nobody could say Andy didn't do that.

The amount of respect he continued to show her was sometimes a worry to Debbie. So far, the most intimate thing they had done was sit on a couch and indulge in some very light necking. Other girls – less sensitive girls, of course – might have interpreted this as a lack of sexual interest on Andy's part. Debbie made a steady effort to keep things in perspective; he was clearly very fond of her and had even managed to tell her so, therefore he had to be interested in her physically. He certainly wasn't repelled. For her own part, Debbie was every bit as fond of him, and she was certainly keen enough to know more about his manhood. So to speak.

She had told no one that she was still a virgin. Not even Andy, in case he found the responsibility of being First Man There too much to handle. All along, right from the time she began to understand the score with couples, she had sworn she would never have sex with any man unless they were going steady. Her principles,

118

plus her occasionally severe manner, had ensured that no boyfriend lasted more than a week or two, until Andy came so dramatically into her life.

Their relationship was precious to Debbie, but it hadn't gone the way her daydreams had painted it, years in advance. She had imagined at least *some* careless rapture. Instead, the courtship remained almost as it had begun; rather stilted, with much serious talk at times, a lot of walking in the good weather, drinks and entertainment at weekends only. There was certainly no larking about. By some people's standards, it would be judged an odd arrangement. Andy always came over and visited Debbie – he didn't like her travelling on public transport at night. They were seldom on their own, indoors or out, and not once had Andy suggested, by word or deed, that he would care for even a little more intimacy between them.

'That Andy looks like he can certainly put his back into his work,' one of the girls at the flat had remarked, with the inevitable smirk.

'Handy looking big chap,' the other female flatmate had commented.

The head cashier, Cynthia, had put it more bluntly. She had seen Andy one evening when he waited for Debbie outside the bank. Next morning she delivered her oblique verdict as Debbie passed through the secure area towards her own department; 'No wonder you look knackered these mornings.'

Debbie never confirmed any of the wilder assumptions about the relationship, but she denied none of them, either. At least people believed she was having a high old time, and a lot of girls openly envied her. Appearances were being maintained, and that had always been important to Debbie. If there were little problems, small worries, they would sort themselves out. The important thing to remember was that he was definitely the man for her. She felt very lucky to have found him.

One morning in October, an otherwise bright, pleasant day, Andy found himself staring down both barrels of Sister Meldrum's wrath. He had been called to the office and as soon as he entered the little woman went for him.

'What kept you?' she demanded. She was standing behind her desk, one hand magisterially propped on her hip. 'I sent for you over three minutes ago.'

'I was about to administer an injection, Sister. I couldn't stop just like that.'

'It's not an impossibility.'

'The child was distressed enough,' Andy explained patiently. 'It would have been cruel to put her through all that twice.'

'Shut the door.' She watched closely as he obeyed, as if she might detect a fault in the way he performed the action. 'Right.' She tapped a sheet of paper on the desk. 'Reginald Moore. Do you remember the case?'

At first Andy didn't, then it came to him. Little Reggie. Five years old, a cheery lad with big inquisitive blue eyes and a shock of blond hair. He had been admitted suffering from congestive heart failure.

'I remember, Sister. He died about a month ago.'

'You made several entries on his case sheet. You also administered treatment.'

'That's right, I did.'

'You also committed a major breach, which I'll come to in a minute.'

'A breach? How?'

She ignored him. She was staring at the record. 'You also appear to have invented some new medical abbreviations, Nurse.' Sister tapped the paper again. 'I've been

120

making a review of ward case-sheets before they're filed.' Her expression switched suddenly. 'I'm shocked, *disgusted*, at your lax approach to routine record-keeping. If it were my only complaint it would be complaint enough.'

'I don't understand – '

'I'm sure you don't. Your lack of understanding might explain some of the blunders and omissions – '

'It's what you're talking about that I don't understand, Sister.'

She glared at him, her eyes appearing to bulge. 'Really? An example, then.' She picked up the sheet and read from it. '"Probable cause of condition established by Consultant as Bend." Now what does that mean?'

Andy looked blank. 'Can I see it?'

Sister thrust the record at him and he looked. He found the entry at once. It read b.end., not bend. He pointed that out to Sister. 'It's a standard abbreviation for bacterial endocarditis.'

She snatched the paper back and looked. 'You'd need pretty good eyesight to see the full stop.'

Andy sighed. 'It looks the same every time I write it,' he said. 'It's not as if that's a crucial part of the report, anyway. It's only a preamble.'

'It's an indistinct feature of the preamble.'

'You never complained before.'

'Don't be insolent.'

Andy swallowed his sudden anger, though he didn't lose it.

Sister's eyes were roaming across the sheet again. 'Ah. Yes. Here. Digoxin. You've spelt it wrong. You put an "e" on the end.'

Andy didn't believe his ears. 'I do that sometimes, I have to admit,' he said acidly. 'It's a bit like the way you occasionally spell my surname in the day book with an "a" instead of an "e". We're all fallible.'

'We're talking about a medical record here!' she practically screeched.

He nodded. 'Fair enough. But before we get too far past the topic, would you like to tell me the other abbreviations I've apparently invented?'

She blinked, her cheeks purpling. 'What?'

'You said I appeared to have invented *some* new medical abbreviations. Some is plural.'

'I'd remind you of your position here, O'Brien, and kindly remember mine while you're at it.'

'I see. There aren't any other abbreviations you find fault with.

Furious, Sister glared at the sheet, her eyes darting as if they had been over-lubricated. The finger stabbed again. 'Here it is,' she growled with dark triumph. 'The whole reason I called you in. This is unforgivable.' She cleared her throat and read, '"Dosage of Digoxin, ten microkilograms daily. Higher doses should be avoided to prevent damaging renal blood flow."' When she looked at Andy her face was suffused with a replica of holy fury. 'How *dare* you?'

'How dare I what?'

'You mean you don't know? Well then Staff Nurse O'Brien, if that's the case, I can see there'll have to be a drastic re-evaluation of your competence for the job. I'd have thought – '

'Tell me!' Andy barked suddenly. 'Tell me what's wrong there, and tell me now!'

'Don't you shout at me!'

'Sister Meldrum . . .' His voice had gone low, but he was still angry. 'You've got me in here, on the carpet, in

122

the middle of a busy morning, just so you can blow your top over a load of nothing.'

'Not one more word – '

'Listen!' he snapped. 'You've not been content with doing that. You've gone on to cast doubt on my professional ability. Well, if what you've just read out is your proof, you're going to find *yourself* on a carpet, somewhere over in Admin. Because I'm not taking this from you. Got it?'

Sister's fingers closed in a spasm, crushing the corner of the paper. 'You . . . You . . .' It was a choking noise, the outward gurgling of a rage too inflexible to mould itself to words. Again she stabbed at the paper and kept doing it until she could speak. 'You deny this is an evaluation? You specifically warn against increasing the dosage . . . That is *not* for you to decide! It isn't your province! The breach is gross and arrogant and it will be punished with the utmost severity!'

Andy had become swiftly detached from his anger. Sister had become pitiful, despicable in her pettiness. He watched her froth like a Calvinist, trying to exercise a power of dread authority she had never possessed.

'Can I see that again?' Andy extended his hand and she slapped the paper into it. He read for a moment, then nodded. 'Your own oversight could put your personal powers of judgement in the very strongest doubt.' He looked at her. 'I'm the only witness to what you've said and to what you've overlooked, of course.' Before she could say anything he added, 'And you're the only witness to what I'm saying, Sister.'

She looked as if she would like to hit him. 'What oversight?'

He read from the same section of the notes as she had.

'"Dosage of Digoxin, ten microkilograms daily." That's what I wrote, Sister.'

'The rest,' she hissed, 'that's what I'm on about!'

Andy looked at the next phrase, heavily inked in capitals; HIGHER DOSES SHOULD BE AVOIDED TO PREVENT DAMAGING RENAL BLOOD FLOW. He looked at Sister. 'What about it?'

'It's a clinical evaluation! It amounts to the kind of judgement you are forbidden to make on any medical record!'

'Yes,' he nodded. 'It is an evaluation. And it's Dr Norris's.'

'Don't try to wriggle out of this . . .'

'He wrote that,' Andy said calmly. 'You can check my capital letters in other reports. They're nothing like these. And see that?' He held the paper under her nose. 'The little squiggle underneath? I'd have thought you'd recognize Dr Norris's initials.'

She snatched back the document and stared at it. She went on staring.

'Do you mind if I go now, Sister?' Andy said wearily. 'I've important things to do.'

She said nothing. Her eyes were still on the paper. Andy turned and walked out.

At break time he saw June Reilly sitting alone in the canteen, her cape wrapped snugly about her. He got a coffee and sat down opposite her. 'I fancy Beattie's snapped,' he said.

'Has she had a go at you, too?'

'You mean I'm not the only one?'

June shook her head. 'She had me in the office first thing.'

'But you're on Paediatric Outpatients this week . . .'

'It didn't stop her sending for me. I got a bollocking for leaving two syringes where patients could get at them.'

Andy frowned. 'Where did you leave them?'

'On top of the drug cupboard.'

'What?' The cupboard wasn't even in the ward. If it had been, it would still have taken a very tall child to reach up to the top. 'That's crazy.'

June nodded. 'My note-taking came in for a bit of hysterical criticism, too.'

'Snap.'

Andy told her what had happened. She didn't appear to be surprised.

'Seriously, June, I think she's going up the twist.'

'No, it isn't quite that,' June said slowly. 'She's going down, Andy, and she's trying to take as many down with her as she can, or at least harm them in passing. She's behaving irrationally, I'd say, but she's not insane yet.'

'Going down? How d'you mean?'

'The grapevine got through on the blower ten minutes after she'd finished with me. I understand she's been upstairs and they've had a short sharp talk with her. She has the option of moving to the Geriatrics Unit on the other side of the borough, or resigning.' June lit a cigarette before she went on. 'It seems her little thing with Miss Pomphrey has become known to the powers.'

Andy's cup had been halfway to his lips. He put it down again without drinking. 'She can be fired for *that*?' I don't believe it!'

'She can't be done under any official regulations. But she's not likely to try defending herself, is she? It would all have to come out in the open.'

Andy scowled. 'The rotten buggers.'

'So say all of us. Now you know why Beattie's the way she is. She's like a little kid now – powerless against cruel authority, kicking out where she can and while she can. We all know she's a pain in the arse, but . . .'

'She doesn't deserve this.'

'No.' June made a mock-sweet smile. 'What she was up to wasn't quite nice, though, was it? Certainly not natural.' The smile dropped. 'You can see the thinking. There are nurses and doctors in this hospital who regularly do things that would make a pathologist puke, but it happens between men and women, so it's A-OK.'

Andy drank his luke-warm coffee in one gulp. He slapped the cup into the saucer and stared dolefully at June. 'You might not believe this, but I think that by the end of the day I'll be feeling heartbroken for Beattie.' He sighed. 'I'd been looking forward to saving all my pity for myself.'

'What's the matter?'

'I've got to move out of the flat. We all have. There's a so-called irregularity in the lease. Geoff's been gypped to the tune of God knows how many hundred quid, and we're all effectively homeless as from the end of November.'

'Shit.'

'I suppose I'll go back to the residency for a while. Can't find anywhere round here at this time of year. Anywhere else would cost more, anyway. I can't afford it.'

'Why not move in with the girlfriend?'

'We're not ready for that yet.' It was a convenient, impromptu answer to a question he had never even considered. 'Anyway, she lives too far away.'

'Try not to feel too sorry for yourself.' June stood up. 'Things could be worse.'

'Oh, they are,' Andy assured her. 'I'm going round to meet Deb's parents next week.'

'God, is it that serious, then?'

He shrugged. He didn't really know the drill. He'd suspected most boyfriends went to meet the girl's folks at some time or another. He just didn't know.

'Don't get too depressed. Think of poor old Beattie and count your lucky stars.'

'I will.'

When June had gone he bought another cup of coffee and went to stand by the window. It was terribly odd, he thought, gazing out over the grubby roofs of Walford. Ten minutes ago, he'd been prepared to put down the roots of a virulent hatred for Sister Meldrum. Either that, or nourish the conviction that she was certifiably insane. Now, apprised of the facts, he felt his sadness for her welling stronger by the minute. No wonder she had wished him harm; no wonder she probably wished the whole world harm.

On his way back to the counter with his empty cup he decided that, whatever else, his capacity for charity was coming on a bundle. There had been a time when he would have been glad, even vengefully gleeful, about what had happened to that spiteful, vindictive, ill-disposed old cow. Now he didn't have even a last trace of dislike for her. Only compassion.

'Poor old Batty Beattie,' he murmured, striding out into the corridor. He would try to find something nice to do for her. Something that wouldn't put her at his throat.

13

'I must say I'm still surprised, Debbie.' Iris Wilkins pulled a duster from the pocket of her wraparound apron and flicked one of the brass-look candlesticks on the mantelpiece. 'A whole year and more. I'd have expected you to say something about him before now.'

'She did say somethin' about him before now,' Derek pointed out, winking at Debbie. 'She told us a couple of weeks ago.'

'You know what I mean.' Iris pocketed the duster again and started undoing the apron. 'What was so secret you couldn't tell us?'

'No secret. I just take these things seriously, Mum. I wanted to know this was working out.'

Iris waggled her new hairdo, a pile of loose curls that looked as if they belonged to somebody else. 'It took you that long?'

'Just accept things,' Debbie told her mother. 'I've been seeing Andy regularly for a while now, and I decided it's time you met him. In about ten minutes you will.'

Iris took her apron out to the hall cupboard and hung it up. When she came back there was a new misgiving wrinkling her brow. 'I wouldn't have thought there was much future for a man in nursing. Does he make much?'

'Iris,' Derek chided softly. 'Debbie's not a school kid. Stop quizzin' her.'

Iris disappeared again, into the kitchen this time.

'You'd think Prince Andrew was comin',' Derek murmured.

Debbie shook her head. 'She'd prefer it if Prince Andrew was coming, you mean.'

'Yeah, I s'pose so. She's had her barnet done an' put on her best frock. She's hoovered the place till there's damn near no pile left on the carpets, she's dusted an' polished . . .'

'I knew she'd go over the top,' Debbie sighed. 'She's always got to give a superior impression of herself.'

'She hasn't met one of your young men before. It's a bit of an event. I must say, I'm lookin' forward to meetin' him, an' all.'

'Mum would have preferred me to bring round a lawyer, or maybe an insurance broker. Male nurse isn't one of the names on her list of desirable professions.'

Derek laughed softly, shifting in his chair for comfort. 'She's got to have her dreams, Debbie. These twenty years she's been watchin' the horizon. It's no nearer, it never will be. But it's somewhere to keep her sights fixed.'

'And a little thing like reality won't make her change.'

The history of Iris's aspirations and hopes was a permanent backdrop in Debbie's memory. When she was very young her mother formulated a plan; Debbie would never have to go through life dependent on other people – not for handouts, not for the right to eat, not for anything. When Derek was injured and could no longer work, Iris took jobs as a cleaner and a school-dinner lady. She provided, and took nothing for nothing. She instilled in her daughter the value of independence, making herself a salutary example. She drove Debbie – overseeing and checking her homework, monitoring her friends, insisting that she took part in all major sporting events at school – laying the groundwork for the full, competent, self-steering woman.

Debbie had never forgotten the day it all came together. At the age of sixteen, out of school and armed with her CSEs and O Levels, she found that her hard-won strands of self-reliance had suddenly became her lifeline. Her mother told her she was on her own – 'I've taken you so far, now it's up to you. From here on I have to look after your father.'

Derek looked at his daughter now and nodded approvingly. 'You're lookin' real smart, love.'

'Thanks, Dad. It's my social-occasions gear.' The silky blue dress with the Greek top and slender silver belt had been a gift from Andy. 'I thought Mum might get a bit moody if I turned up in jeans.' She appraised her father. 'You're looking pretty dapper yourself.'

'Your mum. She insisted I put on me pullover an' a tie.' He glanced at the clock. 'Why didn't he come with you?'

'He doesn't finish till six today. He told me to come on ahead, instead of hanging about at the flat. He's got the address, I don't think he'll get lost.'

'As long as he's not late,' Derek said quietly, so that Iris wouldn't hear. 'She's worried the top of the lemon meringue pie'll go soggy if it sits too long.'

At three minutes past seven, as the tension in the small living room began to mount, there was a sharp rap at the front door. Iris immediately touched her hair. Debbie shot to her feet and went into the hall, casting a glance behind her. She saw her mother rise and smooth her dress. Her father was straightening his already-straight tie.

When Andy came into the room behind Debbie, four separate expressions collided. Iris's smile of welcome couldn't mask her analytical stare; Debbie had a nervous, frozen-eyed look; Derek's bright anticipation was the exact opposite of Andy's gaunt apprehension.

When the introductions had been made Andy produced a gift-wrapped box from his pocket.

'A little something, Mrs Wilkins . . .'

It was only then that Iris realized he was Scottish. At first, judging from the couple of clipped how-d'you-do's, she had thought he might be Welsh. As she took the little parcel and tore at the paper, she wondered why Debbie hadn't mentioned his nationality. It was terribly important, after all. The man came from another country. A considerate daughter would tell her parents that, just to give them some warning.

'Oh. Chocolates. Thanks very much, Andy.'

'Debbie told me you liked them.' He produced another packet, less florally wrapped. 'Mr Wilkins . . .'

'Oh, my word . . .' Derek managed to tease off the Sellotape while the others stood watching, as if he were opening a lottery prize. 'St Bruno! My favourite bacca. Cheers, Andy.'

'Sit yourself down, Andy,' Iris said. 'I'll just see to the tea and things.' She went off to the kitchen, her small frown suggesting she'd heard a warning somewhere about Scots bearing gifts.

By eight o'clock, in spite of the efforts of Debbie and her father to cut back Iris's drive, the tone of the evening had been set. Quite against his will – and at exhausting length – Andy had to explain and justify his career-choice and prove, against heavy scepticism, that he was doing something worthwhile, and with a future. In spite of everything he said, Iris went on casting doubts.

'But surely it's a job more suited to a woman?'

'It's a job that was started by women, Mrs Wilkins.

131

But a lot of the heavy work's more than a woman should be asked to do, frankly.'

At the centre of the semi-circle around the fireplace, Iris kept switching her eyes to her husband or Debbie each time her questions were being answered.

'Even so,' she said, looking at Andy for as long as it took to deliver her next point, 'the very name – nurse – it has a woman's sound to it.'

'So has cook,' Andy said. 'But the best ones are men.'

Iris bridled visibly. 'What about Fanny Craddock?'

She had lost Andy. He glanced at Debbie.

'What's that got to do with anythin'?' Derek asked his wife sharply. Several times he had tried to get the subject away from Andy's work, but Iris wouldn't be deflected.

'I'm just saying it's an unusual occupation for a man.'

By now, there was a trace of animosity in Iris's tone. Debbie didn't miss it, and she was sure Andy didn't, either. By fairly swift stages, her mother had made it clear that she believed her daughter was selling herself short. Debbie recalled her dad's old saying: 'There's no snob like a working-class snob'. Sensing Andy's growing discomfort, mounting in tempo with her own annoyance, Debbie cut in.

'Andy's in one of the most honourable, dedicated profession's in the world, Mum.'

Iris puckered her lips before she smiled; it made her look as if she had tasted something sour. 'For a woman, yes . . . And I mean, looking after sick children – well, it's a woman's natural work, isn't it?'

'That's a very outdated point of view if I may say so, Mrs Wilkins.' Andy was doing his best to keep his tone friendly. 'The care of the sick is a complex business. It needs patience and application – which you'll find as much in men as in women.'

'When I think of a man tending the poorly,' Iris said, 'I always picture a doctor.' She met his eyes sharply. 'I don't suppose you were able to go into doctoring, were you?'

'When I was sixteen I thought about it.'

Now Iris looked heavily sceptical. 'Really? And you decided not to?'

'I decided I could never afford it. It's not the kind of financial strain I'd have wanted to put on my family.'

Iris nodded. 'I see. It takes a bit of money, I suppose. Your family are working people, are they?'

Debbie couldn't stop herself. 'More middle-class, weren't they, Andy?' As he nodded she looked at her mother. 'Not nearly as hard up as we were, Mum.'

She might as well have clubbed Iris. 'We'd have made any sacrifice to see you got what was best for you,' she snapped.

'Anyway,' Andy said, trying to defuse the atmosphere, 'I'm happy in my profession, and I've plans to move up – although I want to stay in touch with the patients. No administrative appointment for me, if I can help it.'

Suddenly Iris was on a new tack, though her intent didn't shift. 'People's jobs are always interesting to me, I must say. What was it that young man used to do, Debbie? The one from Gillingham that you used to go out with?'

'I only went out with him once, Mum,' Debbie said coldly. 'He was in cabin services with British Airways.'

Iris was nodding. 'That's it. Cabin services. That sounds like an interesting job.'

'It was just a fancy way of saying he was an air steward,' Debbie pointed out. 'You know, a man on a plane doing a woman's work.'

Iris did her best to leapfrog that one. 'But you do hear about so many fascinating professions, don't you?'

'They're all interestin', one way or another,' Derek said. 'Look at my job . . .'

'Yes, well . . .'

'I was in the council roofin' department, Andy. There's a damned sight more to puttin' together a roof than most folk would guess.'

'I'll make us some more tea,' Iris said, shooting to her feet.

At ten o'clock, Debbie finally said they would have to go. The evening had been uncomfortable and protracted. Andy's expression for the final hour had moved between annoyance and exasperation, as Iris energetically kept up her stance of disapproval. Derek had finally been submerged by embarrassment and the desperate need to go to bed. Debbie felt mortified.

At the door, Iris kissed Debbie's cheek and bade Andy a metallic goodnight. 'I suppose you'll have to be up early,' she said sweetly. 'Lots of nappies to change, and all that.'

'That's right. A bit of breast-feeding here and there, too.' He walked away before anything else could be said.

Debbie caught up with him at the corner.

'Andy! There was no need for that!'

He stopped and looked down at her. 'Listen, Debs. If that woman hadn't been your mother – '

'Oh all right, I know, she was a bitch. But that's mothers, isn't it?'

'Is it? I've had a few, but I don't remember any of them being like her.' He began walking again. Debbie had to trot at double pace to keep up. 'Thanks for getting me into that,' he muttered. 'I'd do the same for you, except I don't know any place I could come up with anything so horrendous.'

Debbie stopped. 'That's my family you're talking about!'

Andy stopped and turned. 'I know. To get the record straight, let me say I think your dad's a really nice bloke. By God, he must have suffered over the years – and I'm not just talking about his rheumatism and his disability.'

Debbie actually stamped her foot. It made a sharp, echoing little click on the dark street. 'That's uncalled for!'

Andy took three long steps, bringing himself up close to her. 'Let me tell you something about parents, Debs. It's a personal view, mind you, but it's the only kind I've got. They do nothing that gives them the right to influence your adult life. You owe them nothing and they should expect nothing from you.'

'Oh? And how do you make that out? Didn't all your foster-parents do anything for you?'

'They did it largely for themselves.'

'That's just cynical.'

'It's a clear-eyed assessment. People are feeding a selfish need when they foster a kid, or when they have one of their own. Of course, a lot of children are just accidents, to be coped with. You have to keep the picture straight. Parents don't have an automatic licence to inter-fere. They don't earn it.'

'My mother slaved to see I had everything!'

Andy nodded. 'And she reckons she bought the right to intrude in your life and hand out her third-rate judge-ments whenever she feels like it.'

'That isn't fair!' Debbie was close to tears. 'You make her sound . . . mercenary. It isn't true. She expects nothing. She won't have a penny of help from me.'

'Which keeps you in her debt. Nice touch.' He turned and began walking again.

When Debbie caught up she grabbed his arm. 'Listen. I'm sorry about what happened. If I'd guessed it'd be like that, I'd never have arranged for us to go round there.'

'I believe you. And I accept your apology.' They walked on in silence for a while. At a corner Andy glanced at Debbie. She still looked upset.

'Something wrong?'

'Oh, it's . . .'

'What?'

'Mum. I can't help feeling bad about her. She doesn't mean half the things she says and does. She's just anxious for me, Andy.'

He nodded slowly. 'Set her mind at rest, then.'

'How do you mean?'

'Take a budding bank manager round for tea.'

Debbie stopped. Andy kept walking. Behind him, he heard her hail a taxi. Let her, he thought. There were limits to what he would take without kicking out. It was well beyond the limits for some old tea-lady to tell him that for all his learning, dedication and sweat, he was quite unworthy of her daughter.

14

By the third week in November, the word around the bank was that Debbie Wilkins had become, arguably, the grouchiest, pushiest, most hostile individual on the staff. It was an exaggeration, of course. Most of the time Debbie went about her work quietly, bothering no one. She impressed the manger with her efficiency and the consistently high quality of her work. It was only when small tensions arose, or the occasional disagreement, that Debbie displayed a talent for snapping and biting that had already gained her the nickname of Alligator.

'Watch out for the Alligator,' juniors would say, 'she's in one of her moods.' Or, 'The Alligator's been a bit quiet for a couple of days.'

Living with nerves as taut as bowstrings wasn't easy. Debbie had waited, during the first week after the row with Andy, for the 'phone call which she believed was inevitable. He would get on the line and mumble an apology; she would act huffy for a minute or two. Then, reluctantly she would agree to let bygones be bygones. And that would be that. Things would be back the way they had been.

Except the call never came. After the second week she began to develop the nervous characteristics of someone who had just given up smoking; abstaining from calling Andy was hard, terribly hard at times, but she wouldn't give in. Her temper suffered, and in turn those around her suffered, too.

Unlike the reformed smoker, though, Debbie didn't

get better. The sense of loss was so oppressive that some evenings she would shut herself in her bedroom as soon as she got home, staying there like a grieving widow, not emerging again until morning. Even then she said little to her flatmates. At work she was the businesslike zombie, breaking off, occasionally, to go to the washroom and shed a few bitter tears. Her sense of loss was accompanied by no loss of pride, however. She would *not* call him.

The last week of the month saw Andy under such a pressure of work that he had little time to dwell on heartache. It was there, though, like a hollowness at times and a sharp pain at others; even so, he sternly refused to let himself get in touch with Debbie. He had his pride, after all. And he was desperately busy, too busy to let emotion swamp him.

Sister Meldrum had gone away, without ceremony or even a simple farewell, to nurse Walford's Geriatrics. Temporary responsibility for running the ward fell jointly on Andy and June Reilly. On top of their normal ward duties – which had not been suspended – they had to carry out all the administrative work formerly handled by Sister Meldrum. They also took turns to supervise the three Paediatric Outpatient clinics which were held each week.

On the final clinic morning of the month, Andy found himself struggling under more than the usual clutch of handicaps. He was one nurse short, the appointments clerk had double-booked two of the doctors for their eleven o'clock slots and the crowd in the waiting room, for some reason, was especially unruly. The polished floor and hard-glossed walls threw back sharp echoes of howling kids and shouting women. To a man aching from a buried wound and buckling beneath a good measure of exhaustion, the morning was like an enactment of hell, specially laid on to let him know things could always get worse.

'My Larry's sufferin' enough, without you tellin' me he can't go in for another half hour yet.' A fat woman rebuked Andy. She was wrapped in artificial fur and clutched a sniffling child to the hillock of her bosom. 'His sinuses is killin' him. We was told they'd get washed out this mornin' at eleven sharp, an' God knows the poor mite's been brave waitin' all this time . . .'

'Another few minutes won't make too much difference,' Andy said. 'If you want a coffee while you're waiting there's a machine by the main door.'

'I want what I came for.'

As Andy prepared to put the same reply a different way, another woman tugged his starched sleeve. 'My purse has been pinched.' She was glaring at Andy as if he was the prime suspect. 'Right out of me handbag.' She switched her attention to the fat woman. 'Can you imagine it? In a hospital, of all places. You'd think you'd be safe, wouldn't you? I mean muggin's not what you expect when you walk through that door, is it?'

The purse was eventually found, but only after a full-scale frisking of runabout kids and a search of the litter bins. It was located in the owner's pocket. Without a trace of embarrassment or apology, she let out a whooping laugh, remembering she had put the purse there earlier, after she had bought her Eric a drink.

At eleven-fifteen a well-nourished, muscular boy of ten socked a female doctor for hurting him with her auroscope. While Andy was restraining him, another child in a nearby cubicle kicked out reflexively during an examination and upset an entire trolley of instruments. No more than three minutes later, the brother of a young patient sliced open his hand as he pocketed some disposable scalpels. While emergency repairs were being carried out on the hand, a baby in the waiting room managed to swallow a pom-pom off its jacket.

'Too bloody bizarre for words,' Dr Norris muttered as he crossed the waiting room with Andy. 'Some mornings you'd swear they'd been paid to come in here and annihilate the system.'

Andy was consulting his patient list. 'You've got three extras on here,' he sighed. 'Not my fault, I swear. They've been transferred from Casualty for general check-ups. Two sisters and a brother with minor burns from a house fire. They're all showing signs of malnutrition.'

'Christ.'

'And I'm afraid the social worker wants a word – '

'Talk's all she ever does. Any other surprises?'

Andy nodded. 'They'd like you to pop over to ortho-paedics, when you can. There's a kid with a broken arm who looks like he might be a glue sniffer.'

'And?'

'A lad in Casualty has something wrong with his head movement – '

Andy cut off suddenly and skidded to a halt. He was staring at the row of seats on his left. A woman in her twenties had a small girl by the arm. She was slapping the child's head violently as she shook her to right and left. Dr Norris turned in time to see Andy rush across and snatch the child away. With his other hand he thrust the woman back violently against her chair.

'Cut that out, do you hear?' The place went quiet as Andy's shout cut through the hubbub. 'That's a human being you're bashing the stuffing out of, for God's sake! Do you want her brain as damaged as your own? Is that what you're trying to do?'

Norris crossed smartly and touched Andy's sleeve. 'It's

OK,' he murmured, 'I'll take care of this.' He looked at Andy's face, rigid with anger. 'Go and set up the portable X-ray for me in cubicle four, will you?'

It took Andy a second to react. Finally he tore his glare away from the woman's startled face, absently ruffled the howling child's hair and marched off towards the cubicles.

At noon Dr Norris called Andy into his office. He indicated a chair with a cup of coffee steaming on the desk in front of it.

'You need a break, I think,' Norris said as they both sat down.

Andy sighed. 'I'm sorry about what happened, Doctor. I just can't abide that kind of savagery . . .'

'There's no need to apologize,' Norris assured him. 'You did the right thing. What bothers me is the amount of stress you seem to be under lately. Your reaction in the waiting room betrayed it and so do lots of other things. You're so tense these days I'd swear even your hair's clenched.' Norris paused, watching Andy take a gulp of coffee. 'Is there anything wrong? Or am I prying?'

'Nothing's wrong that I can't handle,' Andy said, rather too quickly. 'Lately, I have to admit, I'm a bit more sensitive than usual to man's inhumanity to man.'

'That's pretty common in over-stressed nurses and doctors.' Norris smiled. 'If there's nothing I can do to help, I'll withdraw my nose from your business. However, while you're here . . .' He settled himself deeper in his chair and propped his knee on the edge of the desk. 'I want to tell you I'm very pleased with you. Were you aware that you were under surveillance?'

Andy didn't know how to take that. 'I've not realized anybody was watching me, no . . .' Surveillance was a word he disliked. 'What was the reason?'

'Nothing sinister. I'll explain briefly, there'll be time for details later. For a year I've been planning a reorganization of our child-care setup. The ward, the clinics, the lot. When you came here a few months ago, you seemed the likely type to administer the new system. Your credentials were splendid and your approach to your work seemed just as impeccable. But I had to be sure. Now I am sure. I have been for a while. I've decided that this is the time to tell you, since you could obviously use some bucking-up.'

'Well. It's a bit of a surprise, I must say . . .'

'It's no criticism of Staff Nurse Reilly to say that she wouldn't quite do for the job. She's not one hundred percent into children's nursing. Her heart's elsewhere, she admits it. You, on the other hand, are as close to a true nursing specialist as I've encountered in quite a long time. You're good at the job and you like it. So. Do you feel up to taking overall nursing control on our unit?'

It was the last thing Andy had expected. When he thought about it at all, he had seen his future on the team as a slow-rising spiral, with promotion coming by almost invisible stages.

'I have to say, Dr Norris . . . I don't much like administration . . .'

'Which is why there will still be a Sister on the Ward. And over here. You'll be a full-time nurse, with room to exercise your initiative.'

Andy pictured it. 'That sounds marvellous,' he said.

'It's no more than you deserve. We should be ready to implement the new system by January. In the meantime I'll keep you posted on what's being organized. I'll expect you to suggest any modifications you may think necessary.'

'I'm very grateful.'

Norris sat up and clasped his hands on the desk. 'As I said, you're not getting anything you don't deserve.' He smiled. 'You've even shown an agreeable tendency to fall in with my point of view on the matter of social compassion – not that I wanted to force it on you.'

Andy felt he should declare himself on that point. 'I don't know if I do share your view,' he said. 'I've given it a lot of thought over the months. I've compared what I feel with how I act. Things aren't clear cut or logical . . .'

'They seldom are. Life and logic have very little to do with one another.'

'But I don't have a fixed point of view, Doctor. I mean, look at the way I blew up at that woman out there. At another time I might have acted differently . . .' He shook his head. 'I've no policy that I can consult when I'm dealing with people. I'm guided by . . .' Andy shrugged. 'I don't know.'

'Are you worried that your feelings contradict each other?'

'Exactly.'

'Andy . . .' It was the first time Dr Norris had used his first name. 'You needn't worry about that. Just trust your instinct. From what you've just said, I believe you have something that's every bit as good as a strictly-ordered moral stance.'

'What?'

'Your unwavering humanity. I'd guess you follow the instinct that makes for the greater good, in each case. It isn't the most scientific approach for dealing with anything – but it works very well for you, I'd say.' He held out one flattened hand, as if the concept were sitting right there, clearly visible on his palm. 'Look, I have a standpoint to rely on, right? With you its good intentions. There's no evidence that one is any better than the other.'

Later, as Andy went back to the waiting room, he realized he felt better than he had for weeks. His professional pride, always precarious, seemed very well anchored, for the moment. The prospect of his new appointment excited him, too. But most of all he was elated to know that, in the view of Dr Norris, he was a man of steady goodwill, in spite of feeling murderous at times.

That night Geoff Mercer, Ralph Dixon and Andy had a farewell booze-up in the local pub. In two days they would be out of the flat; Geoff was going to move in with an uncle in Islington, Ralph had scrounged the six-month tenancy of a room in one of the communal dwellings near the hospital, and Andy had already moved most his things into the King George VI residency.

It was a maudlin party. Bereft of the easygoing security of the flat, none of them felt too optimistic about the future.

'My Uncle's a nice bloke, Geoff said, his speech slurring on his fifth pint. 'The house is nice, too. Very tidy and orderly.'

'That won't suit you, will it?' Ralph said.

'Oh, I can learn to put up with anything. Except silence. Uncle Tim's a man of great silences. Just sits there, listening to whatever's going on in his head. He's been like that since Aunt Gloria died. Some nights the place is so quiet you could hear a goldfish fart.'

'Too much racket's what gets me down,' Andy said. 'The residency's going to be hellish. The few days I was there when I first came down, I thought I'd go off my head with the noise.'

'I know what I'm in for,' Ralph sighed. 'As soon as Edna finds out there's a couple of women in the place

144

I'm going, she'll kick up buggery. It'll be one row after another.'

'A good chance to make the break, then,' Geoff told him. 'You've been talking about it long enough.'

Ralph shrugged and downed some beer. 'I'm all talk. I don't want to break it up. Edna's grown on me.'

'Like a wen.'

'Now then, Geoffrey, let's not be too harsh on the girl. In her horizontal moments she's a gem.'

Geoff was looking at Andy. 'Any sign of a reconciliation on your romantic front, mate?'

Andy shook his head. 'None.'

'Have you been in touch?'

Andy looked indignant. 'I'm not going crawling to her, if that's what you mean.' That didn't reflect what had been in his head for the past hour. If he should follow his strongest instincts, like Dr Norris told him, then there was a really strong one that was long overdue for following. 'If I was all that important to her, she'd have been in touch with me before now. It's been a month or more. I reckon she's found somebody else.' He hoped, devoutly, that she hadn't. 'I've more or less written her off.'

Throughout the next two rounds of drinks they reminisced about funny things that had happened during their time in the flat. In retrospect, though, the events were less funny than nostalgically touching.

'Aw, damn,' Ralph said at length. 'I was looking forward to another good Christmas there. That's what's going to hurt most. Having my Christmas expectations cancelled.' Andy felt the same. He'd had his own dream of Christmas. For a couple of weeks he had been trying to bury it for good.

In silence they had one more drink, looking around them, each caught in his private thoughts. Finally Andy emptied his glass and stood up. 'I've something to do, lads. You'll have to forgive me. If I don't go and do it now, I won't be capable.' He swayed. 'I hope I can hold up.'

'I'm off, anyway,' Geoff said. 'Had enough.'

Ralph nodded. 'Drink's for celebrating with. It never was any good for drowning sorrows. The bastards float.'

They parted at the pub door. Andy found a taxi and gave the driver the destination address carefully, trying not to sound too drunk. As the cab whisked him through the glittering night, he felt his head swim. How many pints had it been? Seven? Eight? And there had been a couple of shorts. That was maybe a bit too much, but on the other hand it had taken that amount to make up his mind, so there was no point regretting the excess.

Outside the big front door he took a deep gulp of air, smoothed his hair and hoped his breath didn't smell too strongly. He pressed the bell twice and waited.

The door was opened by Debbie. She was in a cosy-looking blue dressing gown. Her hair was tied up, making her look very young and vulnerable. She stared at Andy.

'Hello, Debs.'

Her eyes didn't flinch. 'You've been drinking.'

'Yup.'

It was hard to read her face. She was masking whatever she felt. Either that, or she really was as annoyed as she looked.

'What are you doing here?'

'Freezing my backside off, actually.' He shivered and looked along the street. 'Can I come in?'

It looked as if she was going to shut the door, but she was merely holding its edge to keep it from blowing shut as she moved back. Andy stepped inside, feeling himself sway again.

She wasn't alone. The two other girls were in front of the TV set in the sitting room. One of the men was in the kitchen. 'We'd better go to my room,' Debbie said.

As she closed the door behind them her face became a little harder. Andy stood looking around. He had never been in here before. Everything was pink and soft and terribly feminine. And tidy. God, he thought, wasn't she *tidy*.

'So.'

Andy turned. Debbie had her back to the door, hands clasped in front of her. 'It's nice to see you,' he said.

'Why did you come?'

'I . . .' Why had he come? Instinct. He'd followed the instinct, instead of avoiding it. Logically, strategically, coming here was a bad move. It showed weakness, and a woman liked to find a niche of weakness and prise it open until it was a big yawning hole. Everybody knew that. But sod the logic and the strategy and the risk, he thought. 'I felt like coming. I wanted to.'

'I see.' She moved away from the door and stopped halfway to the dressing table. 'It took you long enough.'

'Pride,' he said. 'My pride kept me away.'

'Or you just weren't drunk enough, before now.'

He shrugged. 'There could be something in that.' He believed that if he stood still too long he would begin swaying again. He took a step towards her. 'Debbie . . .'

Miraculously, startlingly, her face melted and she came to him, arms outstretched. In a flurry of movement they were embracing, squeezing, mumbling against each other's warmth.

'Oh darling, darling, I've missed you so much,' Debbie moaned, squirming closer. 'So terribly much . . .'

Losing himself in the surge of relief, the heady closeness and the sudden reeling sensation, Andy clung tight and

147

realized he was moving. He was being guided, he wasn't doing this by himself. Not that it mattered. It was glorious, a free-falling swirl of instinct, her scented hair against his mouth, her hands on his back . . .

'Andy . . .' Her mouth was very close to his ear, her breath hot. 'Andy . . . I've never done it before . . .'

It was a shock, though not a sobering one, to discover they were lying across the bed. His hand, he discovered, was on Debbie's unfettered breast. What had happened? He drew back his head and looked for one blinding second. Her gown was open. She was lying pliantly naked beneath him. Drawing back would have been more of a challenge than going forward. He sank down, his hands moving. Another instinct was surfacing in him. It was one he never dreamed he possessed.

Their lovemaking was a frantic, accelerating collision of bodies, mouths, flying fingers and sudden, synchronizing need. Vaguely, through the singing in his ears and the pounding in his chest, Andy was aware of Debbie's legs bracketing his sides, her hips driving at him.

'Andy,' she groaned hoarsely. 'Oh, darling . . .'

He felt her shudder and an instant later his own spasm took him, shaking his entire body as he lunged with tender violence against his whimpering girl.

When it was over they lay still for a long time, holding each other, kissing softly, breathing on each other's faces. Andy believed he had experienced nothing less than a personality shift. He didn't feel like the person he had been. Beside him, Debbie smiled into the crook of his shoulder, glad beyond words.

'Well,' he said finally, pushing himself up on one elbow, running a finger along her neck. He couldn't believe he felt this calm, so completely free of his old reticence.

'Well what?' Her face had softened so much. Her eyes looked liquid.

'This changes a few things.'

Debbie smiled. 'I'll say.' She pulled down his head and kissed him. 'It changes everything, if you ask me.'

He smiled back at her, feeling wonderfully light and carefree. 'Christmas arrived a bit early this year, didn't it?'

15

June Reilly's secret talent came into the open just one hour after the New Year's Eve party began. Like any nurse who kept areas of her life strictly private, June had been the subject of regular speculation among the men – and several of the women – on the staff at King George VI. Without any hard evidence, it was generally believed that when she wasn't working or making an appearance at this or that party, June indulged in something racy enough to keep her as cheerful as she usually appeared.

The party was held in the two adjoining blocks housing the outpatients' clinics. It was, as always, an unofficial gathering. The administration never approved any such celebration, but when it took place, as it always did, there were too many big-wigs present to make it worth anyone's trouble raising a complaint.

June made her revelation at twenty minutes to midnight, amid a rattle of talk and laughter and the blaring taped sounds of UB40. Assisted by two porters, June wheeled in a trolley with a sheet-covered load on top.

'Right, everybody,' she cried, 'quiet please. Please! A bit of hush!'

The music was cut and people gathered round. June stood by the trolley with one corner of the sheet in her hand. She was resplendent in a gold-glinting white dress and elaborately styled hair that had been treated to give an identical gilt sparkle.

'This year, thanks to my efforts and no one else's, the usual mid-party drought will not occur. After two long years of preparation and tender loving care, I'm delighted – and desperately proud – to present the entire 1982 vintage of Chateau Reilly.'

She whisked the sheet aside to reveal a crammed collection of bottles and demijohns filled to the top with light amber wine. There must have been at least ten gallons. The spontaneous roar of approval penetrated the walls and travelled as far as the emergency theatre at the other side of the hospital, where a startled surgical team paused in what they were doing and stared at each other over their masks.

'My God, would you look at that.' Dr Norris shook his head in open wonder. He turned to Debbie and Andy, who were standing beside him. 'Nurses never cease to amaze me.' As June came forward with an armful of bottles and handed him one, Norris placed a kiss on her cheek. 'I had no idea,' he told her. 'How long have you been a wine-maker?'

'Just two years,' she said. 'I took a lot of advice, of course. One of my friends is a biochemist, another one's an alcoholic. One way and another, I've had expert guidance.'

'So this is your first batch?'

'Yes. But don't be nervous. I've been running quality checks on it for a year. That's why my eyes look like perspiring sphincters some mornings.' She gave Andy a bottle. 'To be absolutely sure it's OK, I had the crowd in the Dispensary test it for toxic content.' She pointed to a pharmacist and his two assistants leaning by the door. 'They haven't drawn a sober breath for weeks.'

'What did you make it from?' Andy asked.

'You'd rather not know.' June paused to help one of the porters pass a demijohn over people's heads towards some clamouring housemen near the back of the crowd.

When she turned back to Andy she said, 'It's got nothing artificial in it, take my word for that. Every ingredient I put in there occurred by itself in nature.'

'Tetanus occurs naturally,' Dr Norris said.

'Yeah.' June winked as she moved away. 'There's nothing like living dangerously, huh?'

It turned out to be an agreeable wine – dry, fruity and high on alcohol. By five minutes to twelve a quarter of it had gone. As June and her porters moved the remainder aside for safe keeping until after midnight, Norris said, 'I've a feeling this is a farewell gesture.'

At twelve, as the first chime of Big Ben rang out over somebody's pocket radio, Debbie turned to Andy and clasped her arms around his neck.

'Happy New Year, darling!'

'Happy New Year, Debs!'

All around them people were taking liberties that would be discreetly forgotten by morning. A maternity Sister was limpeting her mouth on the cheek of her senior gynaecologist; in a recess by the drinks-vending machine Geoff Mercer was devouring the mouth of a blonde physiotherapist while he held on like a drowning man to her buttocks; as an avowed act of gratitude, three doctors were kissing and holding various parts of June Reilly.

'They know how to enjoy themselves,' Debbie murmured, still clinging to Andy's neck.

'Amateurs,' he grunted, drawing her close, practising what Debbie called his body-braille. 'Fancy going home?'

She pulled her head back and stared at him. 'I thought we were going to stay here for a while?'

He shrugged. 'Just an impulse,' he said, giving her an extra hard squeeze.

The impact of sex, coming late on the tracks of love, had been both a reversal of the usual pattern and a

152

staggering debut for both of them. It had made a monumental impression that neither one could adequately describe. During their period of separation, they had never seriously doubted they loved one another. Put to the test, that bond had strengthened, making sex a powerful, devastating bonus that got better and richer as time passed.

'You're only after me for my body,' Debbie giggled, drawing away from Andy and picking up her plastic cup, which was half full of wine. 'Randy Andy.'

'I admit it,' he sighed. 'The pleasures of the flesh are reducing me to a husk.' He grinned. 'It feels marvellous.'

For a month they had gone to bed together at every opportunity – though that wasn't nearly often enough for Andy. Although Debbie hadn't said so, she also believed they needed a lot more time on their own. What she never admitted, even to herself, was that sex was now high on her list of preoccupations; sudden recollections would hit her at odd moments during the day, putting such a strong tingle through her that she was sure other people must sometimes have noticed.

'Let's get a top-up,' Andy said.

The trolley-load of wine had been wheeled out again and people were crowding round, filling cups and glasses. As Andy and Debbie pulled free of the throng, clutching their brimming cups, Mr Llewellyn, the nursing tutor, loomed broadly in front of them.

'Staff Nurse O'Brien,' he said, as if it were a clinical observation. His wild Welsh eyebrows met in a frown. 'You haven't introduced me to your ravishing companion. Or if you have, I've forgotten.'

Andy made the introductions and watched, amused, as the tutor put an elaborate, slow-motion kiss on the back of Debbie's hand. Llewellyn was a man who spent the

153

year in sober, studious pursuit of his vocation. Tonight, he appeared to have abandoned even the superficial trappings of civilized living. He teetered drunkenly, his hair was awry and his shirt was open to the waist, revealing a well-fed protruberance of hairy belly.

'You're not one of the young women I regularly lust after,' he said, openly eyeing Debbie from head to toe and slowly back up again. 'From another hospital, are you?'

She explained that she worked in a bank.

'Oh, dear. Banks.' Llewellyn shuddered. 'Not a suitable topic of discussion on an occasion like this.' He slopped some wine into his mouth. 'Music. Now that's something nearer the mark.'

From his appearance, dishevelled as it was, Debbie supposed he would launch into a monologue about the classics. But he surprised her.

'This stuff . . .' He waved a hand in the direction of the tape machine, which was now playing Dr Hook. 'It doesn't have the *bite*, somehow. Give me Crosby, Stills and Nash every time.' He winked knowingly. 'Sixty-nine was their great year, you know. *Marrakesh Express*. That said it all, as far as I'm concerned. And what about the Pink Floyd?' he demanded. '*See Emily Play* – it got well up the chart in 1967, that did.' He spun away, responding to nothing in particular. Andy and Debbie slipped past him and joined up with Dr Norris and June Reilly. They were by the reception desk, which several people were using as a bar top.

Norris looked at Andy, then raised a questioning eye-brow towards June. 'All right to tell him, is it?'

June nodded.

'Sadly,' Norris said, 'as I astutely predicted a short time ago, Nurse Reilly is leaving us.'

'Oh dear.' Andy looked at her smiling face, so familiar now, so much a part of his daily life. 'I'll miss you, June.'

'And I'll miss you, Andy. I'll miss everybody. But.' She shrugged. 'I have to be realistic. I've been made an offer I can't refuse.'

'Where?' Andy asked.

'The Moss Clinic. I'll be a Sister, at about double the Health Service rate.'

'Well.' Andy was impressed. 'Private medicine, eh? There'll be no holding you now. I'm very pleased for you.' Helped by the wine and the recent flowering of his boldness, he stepped forward and kissed June. 'Congratulations.'

'And congratulations to you,' she said, returning the kiss. 'I understand it's official, now.'

Andy blushed a little. 'Yes, it is. Thanks.'

An hour later, after they had tiptoed through the flat where, in the darkness of the sitting room, someone was making love to someone else, Debbie asked Andy the question she had been bottling up since June Reilly congratulated him.

'Right, tell me now. What's official? What's happening in your career that you haven't seen fit to tell me about?'

They sat down on the edge of Debbie's bed. Andy gazed at her querulous expression for a moment, letting his smile spread.

'I was saving it for a New Year's Day treat. A little something extra to celebrate.'

Debbie compressed her lips, annoyed at the way he was making her hang on. 'What? What is it?'

'Oh, I think I'll save it until daylight,' he teased.

'Andy!'

'Ssh!' He put a finger to his lips and jerked his head at the wall. 'You'll upset their rhythm.'

Debbie drew back a small fist and punched his arm. Andy mimed agony and fell over sideways, pulling her with him.

'Tell me!'

He put his face close to hers. 'Dr Norris is putting me in overall nursing control of the sick kids' unit.'

Her eyes became wide ovals. 'Really?'

'Would I lie to you?'

'But that's marvellous!'

'It sure is,' Andy drawled. 'It fits in with everything else, doesn't it? I mean we're making our plans at just about the right time, by the look of things.'

For the next half hour no more was said. In a silence dominated by their conspiring excitement, Debbie let Andy undress her. Then, as she liked to do, she lay motionless on the bed and watched him take off his clothes. Their lovemaking now was less exploratory; a knowledge of each other made them more confident and much more abandoned. The act was prolonged through stages of mounting, delirious tension. It culminated with a wild surge and a transitory satisfaction of their appetite for each other.

In the soft-breathing aftermath Debbie spoke first. 'I've thought about it all day. I'm absolutely sure we're right.'

'So am I.'

The decision was eight days old. They had decided to put it to the test each day to the end of the year, before they committed themselves to action.

'I'm so sure,' Debbie said, 'I can hardly wait.'

They wanted to live together. The overcrowded flat provided the only opportunities they had to be close. The chaotic, noisy surroundings of the nurses' residency heightened Andy's sense of separateness from Debbie. It was no way to go on, they had decided. But they did not want to get married. Not yet.

The misgivings they shared about marriage were crystallized by something Andy had said a few weeks earlier, 'Living together is something you choose to do. Marriage takes away choice and substitutes duty.'

Choice, the badge of their prized independence, was something neither of them would abdicate readily, whatever the reason. Nor would they do anything to hinder or harm their relationship. Living together was not a compromise; it was an answer.

Now, lying in the darkness and watching the dim shadow-play on the ceiling, Andy pictured the months ahead. 'It'll be a strain, all the waiting.'

'But we won't be waiting,' Debbie said. 'We'll be taking steps. Getting ourselves organized. There's tons to do.'

He nodded. 'True enough.'

They would have to find the right place to live. They wanted a house, not a flat. They wanted an old one that they could renovate and shape precisely to their taste. They would also need finance, and there Debbie's job came in very handy. Bank employees, subject to age, status and a few other conditions could obtain low-interest mortgages. It would mean that the house would be in Debbie's name, but that didn't bother Andy – at least, he was pretty sure it didn't. His major contribution would be on the handyman side. It was something he had never tried, but he looked forward to it, nevertheless, with a lot of enthusiasm.

'When will we set the ball rolling?' Debbie asked, snuggling against his side.

'As soon as we can. This week.'

'I can pick up plenty of estate agents' brochures, eh?

We can go through them and look at the likely properties whenever our free days coincide.'

Andy was silent for a moment. 'Debs, there's a doctor at the hospital – he's a GP, works there one day a week. He was talking about houses the last time I saw him. He was complaining about the way the Victorian squares are being allowed to get rundown . . .'

'Mm?'

'Well, his practice is in one of those squares, and there's a couple of houses there standing empty. He said so.'

She thought for a moment. 'Whereabouts?'

'Walford.'

She sighed. 'I'd be right back where I started.'

'No you wouldn't. You'd be a property owner. Local girl makes good, and does it where the locals can see.'

She dug his ribs. 'All right. We'll have a look at your Victorian heaps, along with all the others.'

After a minute Andy began to drowse. Debbie's voice filtered through to him.

'I'm going to say nothing to my mother and father about what we're doing.'

He surfaced at once. 'Why not?'

'I don't want any interference.'

That pleased him. For her, he had been prepared to put up with the occasional, disapproving presence of Mrs Wilkins. He turned and hugged Debbie, realizing this was a sacrifice of considerable proportions; he was sure she would have liked to involve her mother somewhere along the way.

'Listen, Debs,' he murmured against her ear. 'On this first day of 1984, the first day of the best part of our lives, tell me honestly and truthfully – are you a happy girl?'

'The happiest. I swear. How about you? Happy boy, are you?'

'Happy?' He rolled over suddenly, sliding one leg across hers and pushing himself up on his arms. '*Happy*?' He lowered himself towards her, feeling her shift softly. 'I'll show you just how happy I am, my girl . . .'

16

In late January a letter arrived from Glasgow. It was
written in a careful hand on yellow deckle-edged paper,
which looked much jollier than the sentiments conveyed
by the words.

Dear Andy,
  We were very pleased to get your note. It's always a pleasure
to hear from you and to be kept in touch with what is happening.
  It's specially pleasing to know that you are getting on so well.
You must have made a great impression on them to have moved
up so fast. We both hope you will continue to make good
progress.
  The picture of you and your young lady is very nice. We were
surprised you didn't say anything about her before, but I've no
doubt you had your reasons. Her job sounds like a good one, I
am sure she is very clever.
  I have to say, Andy, that your decision to live together comes
as a wee bit of a shock. I had always expected that you would
meet the right girl and settle down some day, but I never
thought you would do it in this way. I suppose I'm old-
fashioned, but I can't help thinking you're making a mistake. If
you truly cared enough for each other, you would get married,
surely. Was this really your idea? I ask that because I know that
nice boys from decent backgrounds can often be led into error a
bit too easily. Do think it over carefully, son. We raised you
always to do the right thing. Don't let all that go to waste.
Remember that plain decency can always dictate your safe path
in life, so long as you turn your ear from the false voices of
enticement.
  Well, I will close now. Dad sends his love, as always. We still
miss you and we're sad that you haven't been able to come up
and see us yet, or write to us more often. Maybe, if your young

lady agrees, you could pay us a visit before the summer. You are always in our thoughts, Andy. Do take care and remember that it's easy to be swayed by novelties. If you need my advice, I am always here.

Love,
Mum

Andy read the letter twice, feeling how poorly his simple gratitude balanced the couple's abiding love. Their love, their possessiveness, their concern and their suspicion. There was jealousy in there somewhere, too. It was a hard see-saw to keep level, he thought. Better not to try. Without their knowing it, he wasn't their big daft boy any more. He was changed beyond anything they would recognize, apart from his appearance. He was a grown man and, what was more, he was a man in love.

Andy returned the letter to its envelope, for good, and put it in the bottom of a drawer.

17

At the beginning of March Debbie and Andy paid their third visit to 43, Albert Square. Of all the properties they had seen, it was the one best suited to their plans and their resources. The house was wide open for renovation and it was cheap.

It was also depressing. The ill-fitting front door with its grimy, scabbed green paint gave due warning of what lay beyond. The place had been empty for two years; neglect had joined forces with decay. The plaster, floorboards, ceilings and communicating doors were all in serious need of attention. The odours of half-dead air and mouldering timber pervaded every corner and hung in dispiriting little clouds in the cupboards and recesses. Ancient wallpaper with the ghosts of flowers and pale, once-gaudy stripes seemed ready to drop from the walls at a touch.

'Three months and you won't know the place,' Andy said firmly. He stood in the middle of the living room and looked round slowly, noting a dozen tricky jobs in one sweep of his eyes. 'It'll be a struggle, mind you. But it'll be worth it.'

From the sad ruin of the kitchen Debbie made a bright effort to agree with him. 'Hard work, that's all it wants.' She came through and looked at Andy. 'We're committed, anyway. We'll have to make a go of it.'

Confirmation of the mortgage had arrived the day before. Until then, all that had concerned them was that they should be granted the finance. Now that it was a reality, so was the enormous task in front of them.

'We will manage it, won't we?'

Andy detected the tiniest note of defeat. 'Of course we will.' He dug out the drawings from his pocket and unfolded them. 'Look. Just think of this room as a box. That's what it is, after all. Once all the muck's been cleared out, we can impose our own shape and style on it.'

Debbie had looked at those sketches a dozen times. This was the first time, though, that she had seen them in the surroundings they represented, She fingered the paper like one of the faithful handling a rosary. The pictures were her reassurance. This ruin could become that dream of order. Looking at the drawings helped. A little.

'Memory's funny,' she said. 'The last couple of times, I came away remembering the place differently. I've sort of coloured it, made it romantic. But God . . .' She stared glumly at a tangle of thick cobwebs in a cracked corner of the ceiling.

'Debs, it's about as romantic as a leg ulcer. You have to be frank with yourself. This house is Mess City. But it *is* a house, a Victorian terrace dwelling in sore need of restoration – no, it's renovation it needs. Between us we'll turn it into a modern, bright, sunny little home.'

'Will we still be young enough to enjoy it?'

'Oh come on, Debs . . .'

'Sorry. It's just . . . Well, now it's ours, or as good as, I'm starting to have my misgivings. It happens with everything I want badly. As soon as I get it, I start seeing all the flaws . . .'

'Like with me?'

'Don't be silly. You know what I mean.'

'Yes, I do.' Andy folded up the sketches and shoved them back in his pocket. 'Now listen.' He put his arm round Debbie's shoulder and drew her close. 'If it's guarantees you want, I'll give you them. Every plan we've made for this house will be carried out, to the last detail. I've enough enthusiasm to convert three places like this. Just don't worry. And remember . . .' He waved a hand at the dingy walls. 'This can only get better.'

He had invested a few pounds in a Reader's Digest DIY manual. He spent every spare moment with it opened in front of him, absorbing the mysteries of plumbing, bricklaying, double-glazing and damp-proofing. Long experience of practical handbooks had taught him that none of it would be as easy as it looked or sounded, but he also knew that single-minded application could make him prevail over any task, so long as he really wanted to do it.

'A home of our own, Debs. Think of it. How many people have the opportunity to mould their surroundings *exactly* to their hearts' desire?'

She was brightening again. 'I know you're right,' she said. 'I'll be as enthusiastic as you, once we get weaving.' She stepped away and peered into the kitchen again. 'I can just see where the cooker will go, and the work tops, the wall cupboards . . .' She spun to face Andy. 'Where are we going to live while we're working on the place?'

'Aha. I've thought about that. To begin with, I think we should set up camp in the small bedroom. Turn it into a little haven, somewhere we can retreat to at night when we're too knackered to do any more.'

Debbie liked the idea. 'A kind of bedsit. Yes, I could make it comfortable for us. I'm pretty good with tight little spaces.'

'So am I,' Andy leered.

'Dirty devil.' Debbie rubbed her hands briskly. 'Well. As soon as I've signed the contract, we're in. The agent

told me it's all right to move in some stuff meantime –
timber, tools, anything we want, really.'

'I'll get on to that next week. I've got Tuesday and
Wednesday off.' Andy looked at his watch. 'It's a quarter
to one. If you've nothing else planned, I thought we
might spend a bit of time getting to know the neighbour-
hood, since we're going to be part of it.'

Debbie nodded. 'Good idea. Maybe we could drop in
at the pub on the corner – I can wash my hands in the
loo.'

Outside they stood on the pavement for a minute,
looking round the square.

'Any idea who lives next door?' Andy asked.

'A family called Fowler, the agent said. Mum, dad and
two kids. There's a grannie lives with them, too.'

Andy pointed towards the end of the square. 'Dr
Legg's surgery's over there. Not far to gallop in an
emergency.'

'You mean if you saw your leg off while you're making
the odd partition or something?'

'That's right.' Andy took her arm and they began
walking towards the Queen Victoria, the pub on the
corner. Beside it, on Bridge Street, there was the busy
tail-end of a street market. 'We won't have far to go for a
drink either, or for the weekly shopping.'

They paused for a moment and listened to the vendor
on the fruit and vegetable stall. He was yelling his current
bargains and throwing in a reference to the length of his
cucumbers.

'Nice an' firm an' all, missus. Best offer you'll get this
side of Easter.'

By the pub Andy looked up at the narrow sign above
the corner doors:

D. A. WATTS – Licensed to Sell Tobacco,
Beer, Wine & Intoxicating Spirits.

Debbie pointed out that there were a lot of tiles missing from the wall of the building. 'It's a bit tatty looking.'

'There's always two ways of looking at places like this,' Andy said. 'You can take them at face value, or you can look beyond that to the character of the place.'

'I suppose so.' Debbie nodded at the doors. 'Let's have a look at some of the characters, then.'

The bar was doing brisk Saturday-afternoon business. On a stool in the corner an old woman clutched a panting little pug on her lap as she bawled energetically into the ear of another woman, who nodded absently while she sipped a Guinness. Beside them, two men with market-traders' cash bags round their waists were studying the same Daily Mirror. People at tables were talking to each other over five- and six-foot gaps, using their hands to fill in parts of their conversation that were drowned in the noise from the juke box.

The landlord, a tall, lean, hard-eyed man in his thirties, came forward as the couple stepped up to the bar.

'Yes, sir – what'll it be?' His eyes made a quick appraisal of Debbie.

'Two halves of lager, please.'

'Comin' right up.' As he pulled the drinks he was still eyeing Debbie.

'I think you've scored a hit,' Andy muttered.

'So have you.'

'Where?'

'The old dear with the dog. She's gaping.'

As Andy looked the woman promptly turned aside. He noticed that her companion was whispering something to her.

'Very parochial, the East End,' Andy said. 'We're being sized-up.'

'You don't have to tell me, darling. I'm from round here, remember?'

As the landlord brought the drinks, a brassy-sexy woman in a tight white blouse and even tighter blue skirt appeared at a doorway behind the bar.

'Den!'

'Yes, my precious?' the man said sourly, taking Andy's money.

'What've you done with them boxes of serviettes that came in yesterday?'

'Under the stairs, sweetness.'

'Never the same bleedin' place twice, are they?' She shot a fiery glare at the back of the landlord's head and withdrew.

'The wife,' he explained to Debbie and Andy. 'Married all these years an' it still seems like yesterday.' He turned towards the till. 'You know what a lousy day yesterday was.'

Debbie went to wash her hands. When she came back Andy took the glasses to a vacant table. They were sitting down when the door flew open and a fair-haired woman in an overall rushed in. She went straight up to the companion of the woman with the dog.

'Mum – you seen our Michelle?'

The old woman glared at her. 'How could I see her? I've been here the past half hour.'

'Before that, I mean.'

'She was goin' up Bridge Street with young Sharon when I come in.'

'That's marvellous. Bloody marvellous. I tell her to come round the launderette for the shoppin' list at

167

half-twelve, an' what happens? I might as well talk to that dog.'

The dog's owner smiled. 'My Willie would understand every word you said.'

'Settle down, Pauline,' the woman's mother told her. 'Have a drink before the top comes off your head.'

'I've not got time for a drink – unlike some people.' Pauline turned and strode out again.

'All human life is here,' Andy murmured to Debbie. 'All we need now is for Barbara Windsor to come in and give us a chorus of *Sparrows Can't Sing*.'

The door opened again and a tall man poked his head inside. For a moment he seemed unsure about staying, then he came inside, letting the door swing shut.

'Dr Legg,' Andy called to him.

The doctor stared for a moment, then his face cleared. 'Well, hello there. I didn't recognize you at first, without the white jacket.' He came across and leaned down by the table. 'Still looking at houses?'

'We've got one,' Debbie said brightly. 'Number forty-three. Oh, I'm Debbie, by the way. Andy's mentioned you to me.'

Dr Legg shook her hand gently. 'Well, well. This is splendid news. My warmest congratulations to you both.'

'Thanks,' Andy said, rising. 'Let me get you a drink.'

Dr Legg thanked him and said he would have a glass of red wine. He sat down opposite Debbie as Andy went to the bar. 'So tell me, are you looking forward to joining our little community?'

'I think so.' She smiled uneasily. 'It might take a bit of getting used to . . .'

'Oh, they're a good lot, my dear.' He glanced at a shabby-looking man by the corner of the bar who was studiously picking his nose. 'For the most part,' he added.

'It's all very lively.'

Dr Legg nodded. 'That's the keynote. Energy, activity. The people here are agreeably close to the real business of living.'

When Andy came back the doctor launched into a brief, enthusiastic social history of the area. In the space of five minutes, Debbie and Andy learned that the square and the streets around were teeming with people whose life stories might have been plotted by Charles Dickens.

'There are men and women in this area who still maintain traditions and standards that were officially dead before the war started,' Dr Legg concluded. 'It's a kind of cultural ghetto, I suppose – but it's changing. That's inevitable. I'm not glad and I'm not sorry. Things do need to change, but I'll miss a lot of what's beginning to disappear.'

'Well, at least we'll stop one Victorian house falling down,' Andy said.

'Which calls for another drink.'

When he came back a couple of minutes later he winked at Debbie. 'That's got the ball rolling.' He set out the glasses and sat down. 'I mentioned to the landlord that you're moving into the square. The bush telegraph will take care of the rest.'

Almost as the doctor spoke the landlady appeared by the table. 'Hello there,' she said brightly, thumbing a bra strap. 'I'm Angie Watts. I understand you're coming to live here.'

Andy introduced himself and Debbie. 'It shouldn't be too long before we move in,' he said. 'It'll be a bit longer before we knock the place into shape, mind you.'

'I'm sure you'll make a good job of it,' Angie gushed. 'You look like a capable big chap.'

Debbie smiled, recalling what her flatmates had said

when they first saw Andy. 'He's all right, with a bit of firm management behind him,' she said.

'Well, welcome to the square, anyway.' Angie flashed a smile and disappeared again. During the next ten minutes a further three residents came across to offer their welcomes and best wishes. The lady with the dog was one of them.

'Ethel's the name. Ethel Skinner. Anythin' you want, any help about the place or suchlike, I'm the one to get in touch with. Isn't that right, doctor?'

'You're too kind for your own good, Ethel.'

'I'm neighbourly, that's all I am.' She tilted her head at Andy, then at Debbie. She then addressed the panting dog. 'They're goin' to like it in the square, aren't they, Willie?'

'Et!' her friend called gruffly from the bar. 'It's your round.'

Ethel excused herself and went back to her stool.

'I think you're beginning to catch the flavour of the place,' Dr Legg said. He glanced at the clock and sighed. 'I'll have to be off. Pity. I could have introduced you to a few of the people on the market . . .'

'We have to get moving too,' Debbie said. 'There's stuff to get, things to order . . .'

The doctor smiled wistfully. 'Setting up house. It's a real thrill, isn't it? I'd almost forgotten.'

They stood up, took the glasses to the bar, said goodbye to Ethel and the landlord and left. On the street, the man at the fruit and vegetable stall called out to them.

'Hope you'll be happy here, you two.'

'Thanks,' Andy called back. He turned to Dr Legg. 'How did he find out so fast?'

'I told you, the telegraph. It operates at roughly the speed of a nerve impulse.'

170

'An' remember, darlin',' the stall holder shouted. 'This is the place to get your fruit an' veg. Don't let me catch you nippin' round the shops.'

'Right,' Debbie promised, smiling. 'Anything I need, I'll come to you.'

'Oh.' The man's eyebrows shot up and he beamed. 'Nice one. I can hardly wait.'

Blushing, Debbie hooked her arm in Andy's. They walked with the doctor as far as the corner by the surgery, where his car was parked. He offered them a lift.

'No thanks,' Andy said. Debbie frowned at him. 'I think I want to stay here just a little while longer.'

'Right. I daresay I'll see you again before long – either here or at the hospital.' Waving, Dr Legg got into the car and drove off.

'What do you want to hang on for?' Debbie asked Andy.

He turned and looked along the rows of houses. 'I thought maybe we'd just walk round the place for a wee while.'

'To get the feel of it, you mean?' She smiled considerately.

'To go on getting the feel of it. I like the vibes round here, Debs. More and more as the time passes.'

'Vibes is an old-fashioned word,' she said. 'You should read more tee shirts.'

'You know what I mean.' He looked at her. 'What do you feel about it? The place, the people.'

What she felt was that the square, quaint in its way, made a perfect setting for the inhabitants, who seemed to embody an almost self-conscious quaintness of their own. She believed Andy saw it rather differently, so she said, 'I like it here. But I could fit in anywhere, I suppose.'

'Best to fit in where it's easiest, though. And here,

Debs – well, I don't think it'll be a struggle.' He began walking towards the little garden at the centre of the square, Debbie strolling half a pace behind him. At the garden he stopped and leaned on the railings. 'Smashing. None of that unlived-in, stiff feeling you get with new places.'

Debbie leaned beside him. She looked across at their house. Its sad little front would be the better for a bright coat of paint, she decided – pale blue, say, with white around the door arch. The chimney looked like it could use some attention, too.

'It hardly seems likely, does it?' Andy said. 'A Scotsman feeling right at home in the heart of the East End. But I do. I'm drawn to the locals, and the place feels familiar already.'

Debbie was sharply aware of the difference in their attitudes. He was defining a spiritual affinity with the place, dwelling sentimentally on his emotional responses; she was preoccupied with the practical issue of creating a fit and decent home. Just as well it was that way, she supposed. He was sprouting the qualifications for harmonious citizenship, while she was concentrating on domestic harmony and wellbeing. A nice mix.

'Are you sure you'll be happy here, Debs?' He was looking at the house now, too.

'Together, we'll be happy anywhere.'

'I think we can make a significant contribution to the life of this district.'

Debbie leaned close to him, smiling. 'You sound like a politician.'

'But you know what I'm on about.' He kissed her hair. 'It's not enough just to live in a place like Albert Square. You've got to slot in and be a living, contributing part of it.'

Andy was thinking about something Dr Norris had said to him, one hectic morning in the Paediatric Clinic. It hadn't been far from his mind since that day.

He sighed and slipped his arm around Debbie's waist. 'It's all down to good intentions, love. We've enough between us to do right by our community.'

Debbie looked up at him. 'Will we have enough left to do right by each other?'

'Tons and tons,' he said. 'You can bank on it.'

He squeezed her, gazing towards the house and across to the busy market. Ethel Skinner had come out of the pub. She set down her dog and untangled his leash. As she began walking towards the square she saw Debbie and Andy. She waved. Grinning, Andy waved back.

The world's greatest novelists now available in Panther Books

Eric van Lustbader
The Ninja	£2.50	☐
Sirens	£2.50	☐
Beneath An Opal Moon	£1.95	☐
Black Heart	£2.95	☐

Nelson de Mille
By the Rivers of Babylon	£1.95	☐
Cathedral	£1.95	☐

Justin Scott
The Shipkiller	£1.95	☐
The Man Who Loved the Normandie	£2.50	☐
A Pride of Kings	£2.50	☐

Leslie Waller
Trocadero	£2.50	☐
The Swiss Account	£1.95	☐
A Change in the Wind	40p	☐
The American	75p	☐
The Family	£1.95	☐
The Banker	£2.50	☐
The Brave and the Free	£1.95	☐
Blood and Dreams	£1.50	☐
Gameplan	£1.95	☐

Peter Lear
Spider Girl	£1.50	☐
Golden Girl	£1.50	☐

Calder Willingham
The Big Nickel	£1.25	☐
Providence Island	£1.50	☐

David Charney
Sensei	£1.95	☐

To order direct from the publisher just tick the titles you want
and fill in the order form.

All these books are available at your local bookshop or newsagent, or can be ordered direct from the publisher..

To order direct from the publisher just tick the titles you want and fill in the form below.

Name _____

Address _____

Send to:
Panther Cash Sales
PO Box 11, Falmouth, Cornwall TR10 9EN.

Please enclose remittance to the value of the cover price plus:

UK 45p for the first book, 20p for the second book plus 14p per copy for each additional book ordered to a maximum charge of £1.63.

BFPO and Eire 45p for the first book, 20p for the second book plus 14p per copy for the next 7 books, thereafter 8p per book.

Overseas 75p for the first book and 21p for each additional book.

Panther Books reserve the right to show new retail prices on covers, which may differ from those previously advertised in the text or elsewhere.